THE BRAVE

THE BRAVE

By
GREGORY MCDONALD

BARRICADE BOOKS • NEW YORK

Published by:
Barricade Books
61 Fourth Avenue
New York, N.Y. 10003

First Edition.
First printing October 1991.

Library of Congress Cataloging-in-Publication Data

Mcdonald, Gregory, 1937-
The brave / Gregory Mcdonald.
p. cm.
ISBN 0-942637-34-8
I. Title.
PS3563.A278B7   1991
813'.54—dc20   91-19312
CIP

Printed in the United States of America

"Must another Christ die in every generation to save those who have no imagination?"
—George Bernard Shaw
"Saint Joan"

"I have observed life carefully, and find it highly indicative."
—Gregory Mcdonald

FOREWORD

THE AUTHOR believes the third chapter of The Brave, Chapter c, is an integral part of the story, that exactly what transpired between "the uncle" and Rafael in that second story loft must be reported fully.

However, the author realizes this chapter is particularly strong and repulsive as it has to do with both immediate, and planned, prolonged human cruelty.

He wishes he could have avoided writing that particular chapter.

The author also believes The Brave justifies the events and circumstances depicted in Chapter c and throughout the narrative generally.

Therefore, the reader is advised that not all will find it desirable or perhaps absolutely necessary to include Chapter c in their reading of this work.

a

"I CAME about the job."

The blue eyes of the heavy young man sitting with his feet propped on the desk first studied Rafael's eyes, then scanned Rafael's thin body.

"Why?"

Rafael shrugged and looked away.

The young man at the desk put down the magazine he had been reading. He put his feet on the floor. A weak smile showed on his slack, gray face.

As if he had not just asked Rafael a question, he asked, "What job is that?"

In the light from the dirty window, Rafael looked around the small office, the single scarred wooden desk and chair, the dented, scratched metal filing cabinet, scuffed floor.

The sign on the frosted glass window on the closed door behind Rafael read: *Enough Enterprises Productions Limited Incorporated*. He had been told the office was up a single, unlit flight of stairs above a certain bar in a street lined with bars.

Rafael asked, "Is there more than one job?"

Still smiling sickly, the young man said, "Only one."

1

"Are you the person I see about the job?" Rafael asked.

"Where did you hear about it?"

"What, the job?"

"Yeah."

"Someone mentioned it to me."

"Who?" The young man asked. "Where? When?"

Rafael shivered. "I'm not a cop."

Again the young man scanned Rafael's faded shirt, worn-out jeans, cracked boots.

"Who?" he repeated. "Where? When?"

"A week ago. About a week ago. Some bar. Some guy."

"What bar? What guy?"

"Freedo's."

The young man nodded. "Just happened to be drinking there?"

"I drink there a lot."

"So who mentioned the job to you?"

"I said: Freedo. The bartender. He's called Freedo. Isn't the place called Freedo's?"

"So you just happened to be drinking at Freedo's and the bartender tells you there's this job?"

"The next morning," Rafael said quietly. "I was still on the floor. He put me in the back room awhile."

"Not the first time, I bet."

Rafael said, "Not the first time."

The young man asked, "You been drinkin' this morning?"

Rafael wiped his dry lips with his thumb. "A little bit."

"Of course you have," the young man said.

"How much does this job pay? I was told twenty-five thousand dollars."

"You got it about right."

"I want thirty."

"My uncle's the one you see about that. I have to see if you qualify first. You workin' anywhere now?"

Rafael shook his head. "Not for a long time now. Long time."

"Why not?"

Rafael's eyes smarted. "Can't get a job."

"Because of the vodka?"

Rafael spread his fingers wide. "There are no jobs."

"Other people have jobs."

"Yeah," Rafael said. "You have a job. You have a uncle, too."

"Haven't you got an uncle?"

"I've got a uncle."

"He hasn't got a job, either, right? Your father hasn't got a job. Your brothers haven't got jobs."

"There haven't been any jobs in a long, long time."

"What did you do when you did work?"

"Helped my brother on a truck."

"What?"

"Helped my brother on a truck. A pickup truck."

"So your uncle didn't have a job for you, but your brother did. What happened? He lose the truck?"

"He still has the truck."

"What he lost is his alky brother."

"There's no work for the truck. Not enough for both of us. There hasn't been in a long, long time."

"You ever have a real job?"

"I've had a real job."

"I mean some place they provide insurance, that kind of thing. You ever paid taxes?"

Rafael exhaled. "I guess not."

"You ever filled out forms, you know, name, where you live, that kind of thing?"

"I guess not."

"Can you read and write?"

"Not real good."

"Married?"

"Sure."

"You got kids?"

"Two daughters. One son."

"How old are you?"

"Twenty-one." Rafael had figured out he had better say he was twenty-one. "Are you the guy I see about the job?"

"Take it easy. Certain preliminaries first."

Rafael said nothing.

"So what about them?" the young man asked.

"What about them?"

"That's why you want this job."

Rafael looked at the closed door in the side wall of the office. "How long do you think I can stand here?"

"I don't know," the young man answered. "How long can you stand there?"

Rafael wondered if it would be all right with the young man if he went and got a drink and came back.

"How many brothers you got?"

"Four. One died."

"Three brothers. All out of work."

"One brother has the truck."

"Any know any cops?"

"No. Not friendly-like anyways."

"Were you in the service?"

"What does that mean?"

"Army?"

"No."

"You've been in jail."

"Sure."

"What for?"

"Drunk."

"What else?"

"Drunk."

"Nothing else? No breaking and entering, mugging, car theft?"

"Drunk."

"Alky your only thing?"

"What?"

"Alcohol."

"Vodka."

"No other drugs? Never been arrested for other drugs?"

"Drunk."

"Where do you live?"

"Calls it Morgantown."

"Morgantown. Guess you wouldn't miss Morgantown, right? Any diseases?"

"What do you mean?"

"I mean, are you dyin' of natural causes?"

Rafael looked at his fingertips. "No."

"You stay right here." The young man got up from his desk. "I'll get my uncle."

Rafael asked, "You mean I qualify?"

b

WHEN THE side door of the office opened, Rafael was leaning against the filing cabinet. From the sound of it, the way it felt against his arm, he knew the filing cabinet was empty.

The uncle came slowly, sideways through the door. His gray, balding head was lowered. He was looking up at Rafael from under heavy lids.

His stomach hung over his belt.

The heavy young man was behind him.

The uncle made a mouth noise, *eruh*, Rafael did not understand.

Rafael stood straighter.

The uncle began to go back through the door. He brushed the young man aside with his forearm.

The young man said to Rafael: "Go with him."

Through the door, Rafael found himself in a huge, dark space. There were small windows along the front and back walls. The windows were so dirty the morning light that came through them was dirty, too.

At a good distance from Rafael, some of the windows along the back wall were covered by black wood or heavy cloth.

In this darker area of the loft he saw a heavy square chair. And there were silhouettes of things each standing on three slim legs.

The uncle was in a glassed-in, lit area in the rear, near corner of the loft.

When Rafael stepped into this area, the uncle looked at Rafael's face. To Rafael, the uncle's eyes, and nose, and lips seemed enormous, all bulging.

"You get a good-looking male Indian, you get a really handsome boy. Man." The uncle looked inside a plastic coffee cup. "You an Indian?"

Rafael did not know how to answer.

The uncle shook a little black coffee from the cup into the metal wastebasket beside his desk. Leaning over with difficulty, he took another plastic cup out of the waste basket and shook it dry, too.

"Alky's your thing," the uncle said. "Trouble with you alkies is you ain't got no asses."

He took a quart bottle of vodka from his desk and poured into the two plastic cups.

"How old are you?"

"Twenty-one."

"Eruh." He handed Rafael the cup he had taken from the waste basket. "You could pass for twenty-seven, eight."

Rafael tossed the drink down his throat. He put the empty cup down on the metal desk.

The uncle lowered his fat body onto a wooden

chair with a semicircular back. The chair was too short for the desk.

"Siddown."

Rafael saw there was a stained, sprung sofa behind him. He found a place to sit on it.

"Can't beat it, huh?" the uncle asked. "Pretty young to know that. Who's to say?" From where Rafael sat, the uncle's head looked much too close to the surface of the desk. "Had any schoolin'?"

"I went to school."

"Lemme see. Quit in fourth grade."

"I was in fifth."

"Drunk even then."

Rafael said nothing.

"Married before you knew it." When the uncle drank his lips seemed to embrace the lip of the cup and draw the vodka out of it. "Did you even know you were married? Suddenly you found yourself married. What is it, three kids? You've been married always, right?"

"I was married by the priest," Rafael said.

"Sure," the uncle said. "They'll always marry you." His lips drew more liquor from the cup. "I agree. It all looks pretty hopeless."

The uncle smiled, then frowned, then looked pleasantly, perhaps happily, at Rafael.

The drink had revived Rafael a little. He was no longer cold and sweaty.

Still he was breathing more rapidly, shallowly

than usual, as if he were getting ready to fight, or to run away.

The uncle asked, "Is this somethin' you're thinkin' of doin' right away? I mean, right now? Is that what you're thinkin'?"

"A few days. A few days from now."

"How do we know you'll come back?"

"I'll come back"

"You'll go get drunk. Stay drunk."

Rafael shrugged.

"We can set things up for you to do it today. This afternoon. All you need is a hair cut. Wouldn't you rather face it, get it over with, do it now?"

"I want thirty thousand dollars."

The uncle said, "You're only worth twenty-five."

"Thirty."

"Twenty-five is what we pay for this particular job. We've never paid more than twenty-five."

"Thirty."

"We can get someone else for twenty-five."

Rafael hesitated. "I don't see anybody else sittin' here."

"We've got time, enough time."

"Then I'll do it in a few days. Not today. And I want thirty."

The uncle stared at him.

"I heard about this job weeks ago," Rafael said.

"Someone's been tellin' me to think about it for weeks now."

"Freedo."

"You want me, it's thirty. In a few days."

"You've never even seen a thousand dollars in your life," the uncle said.

Rafael said, "Thirty."

"I don't know if I want you yet. I have to see your body."

"My body's okay."

"We don't even know if you can get it up."

Rafael said, slowly, "I can get it up."

"Not if there's nothin' in your body but booze days on end."

Rafael knew that was true. "What am I sellin' here?"

"Don't know yet. Haven't looked. You're no good to us unconscious."

"I want a few days to deal with the money."

"What money?"

"The thirty thousand dollars."

"Oh. That's not how it works. You think just because you walk in here and take off your jeans we're gonna give you thirty thousand dollars? That you're gonna walk out of here with thirty thousand dollars in your pocket promisin' you'll come back some time? You think we're crazy?"

Rafael stopped. That was what he had been thinking, more or less.

He thought about it.

"How does it work?"

"Larry will take you to a bank."

"Who's Larry?"

"My nephew. You met."

"What's your name, anyway?"

"McCarthy," the uncle said quickly. "See, Larry will take you to a bank. Ever opened a bank account?"

"No."

"I didn't think so. Ever been in a bank?"

"No."

"Larry will help you. He'll take you to a bank. Help you open an account. In your own name. He'll put two hundred and fifty dollars in your account, in your own name, right in front of you. Cash money."

"Three hundred."

"You get the rest later."

"Later?"

"Afterwards."

"How will I know you've done it? I mean, put the rest of the money in."

The uncle slammed open a desk drawer. He took out a piece of paper and slapped it down, hard, on the desk. He grabbed up a pen and sat poised to write. "Because we're gonna sign a contract, you and me."

Rafael said, "Oh."

"And it's gonna say that if you take this job that after it's over we're gonna put twenty-four thousand, seven hundred and fifty dollars in your bank account."

Rafael could not think what thirty thousand minus three hundred dollars is. "Wrong amount," he said.

"What else can we do? We can't pay you before we do it. You know what a contract is?"

Rafael didn't answer.

"It's binding!" the uncle said. "That means that if we say something, write it down on this piece of paper, and sign it, and you sign it, that means you've gotta do it and we've gotta do it! That's the law! What's your name?"

"Rafael."

The uncle wrote something on the piece of paper on the desk. "Rafael . . ." He slapped the paper and sat back in his chair. "Whadda ya think?"

Rafael did not know what to think.

"You think we're some kind of nuts?" the uncle asked. "We can't pay for a job until it's done. Nobody does." The uncle's voice lowered. He fixed his eyes on Rafael's. "I can already tell from talkin' to you you're a smart boy, Rafael. And a brave one, too, or you wouldn't be thinkin' of this. You tell me: what else can we do? Tell me that."

Rafael had no answer.

"You want the money, don't you? Sure! God!

You wouldn't be here if you didn't want the money. You want the money for your family, your wife and three kids. Somebody sick? Listen, Rafael: this is how you get the money for your wife and three kids. What else can we do?"

Rafael stood up. Gently he put his fingers around the empty plastic cup on the desk. He looked at the uncle in the low desk chair.

"Sure." The uncle pulled the bottle from the desk drawer and poured Rafael another shot.

Rafael took the liquor in one swallow.

He looked the uncle full in the face.

"Thirty thousand dollars," Rafael said.

"Damn!" The uncle slapped the desk with the palm of his fat left hand. "You're smart! You drive a hard bargain, boy!"

"And three hundred dollars at first."

"You mean: up front. In the bank."

"Before."

"I'll be a son of a bitch," the uncle said. "I've never dealt with anybody as tough as you are, boy. As tough and as smart."

Standing there, Rafael felt the fat, bald man was looking at Rafael's body the way some women did.

"First," the uncle said, "let's see what we're buyin'."

C

"**Y**OU MEAN take my clothes off?" Rafael asked. "All of 'em?

"Yeah."

"Here?" He looked around the office and through the glass window into the gloom of the loft.

"Yeah."

"Now?"

"What the hell you think we're talkin' about?" the fat man in the white shirt behind the desk said. "What did Freedo tell you? You're gonna do this thing with us in a jock strap, for Chrissake?"

"Just funny, is all," Rafael said.

Rafael was used to going naked and nearly naked alone and in front of people, his own family and people who had known him since birth. There was something very different about getting naked in an office in the city, in front of this man who did not know him, this man whose eyes bulged at him.

"You care about this?" the uncle asked. "You're crazy."

"I don't care." Rafael sat on the divan and pulled off his boots. "I just can't be all that clean, I expect. My clothes, I mean. I mean, my wife tries. . ."

15

The uncle said, "I know you're a poor son of a bitch. Morgantown. You want another shot?"

"Well, no."

"Take another shot." The uncle poured more into the plastic glass and held it out to Rafael over the desk.

Barefoot, holding his unzipped jeans together with his left hand, Rafael stood by the desk and swallowed another shot of vodka.

"Come on, come on," the uncle said. "I haven't got all day, for Chrissake."

Rafael threw his jeans and shirt and underpants on the sofa.

"Good," the uncle said. "You're a little erect."

"The way you're lookin' at me," Rafael stammered.

First the uncle put the tips of his fingers along the side of Rafael's neck. "Your heart ever act up on you?"

Sometimes Rafael had felt his heart racing when he'd had a lot to drink and wanted more. "No."

"Never had any pains. Ever fainted?"

"Passed out," Rafael said.

"Sure."

"Nearly every damn' day." Rafael grinned.

"That's all right."

The uncle stabbed his forefinger into Rafael's breasts. He lifted Rafael's arm and held Rafael's bicep on his palm. "Shit. Kids can live the way you do and still have some muscle." Bending over, the uncle ran his hand down Rafael's left leg. He then stood back and looked at Rafael's stomach. With a short undercut, he punched Rafael in the stomach and watched the skin redden. He pinched the base of Rafael's stomach and saw how fast the welt disappeared. "The tone of kids' skin," the uncle said. "Christ, it drives ya nuts." Then, walking behind Rafael, he cupped his hand around Rafael's right cheek and stroked it. "Still got some ass, boy. But you won't long, way you're goin'." He stood in front of Rafael and forced open Rafael's lips with his fingers to look at his teeth. "Lousy nutrition," the uncle said. "Ever been to a dentist?"

"Not really. I don't know. I don't think so."

Arms akimbo, the uncle stood in front of Rafael. "You know, Indian, I think you're right to be doin' what you're doin'. A year from now I probably wouldn't even want ya. You'll be totally worthless."

Rafael reached for his shirt.

"No," the uncle said. "Stay naked. Come with me. I want you to know exactly what's gonna happen."

Rafael followed the uncle out of the lit office and along the grimy floor of the loft. He felt the cooler air of the dark loft in his armpits, his crotch.

As they walked, the uncle asked, "You can stand an hour of pain, can't ya?"

Rafael, following, heard him, but didn't answer. He didn't know.

"Sure, you can," the uncle said. "Tough guy like you. You can stand an hour of anything. Isn't that right?"

They went to the area in the loft where the windows were covered by heavy black cloth hanging from the ceiling, where the square wooden chair was, where the strange objects each standing on three slim legs were.

"You ever been in serious pain? I mean, really serious pain?" the uncle asked. He fiddled with something at the top of one of the tripods. "I don't know: some people like it. Bein' in pain, I mean. They actually enjoy it. You might be one of those."

The brightest artificial light Rafael had ever seen flooded the area from the top of the tripod. At first, Rafael closed his eyes and turned his head away.

"Anyway, you want to be in a movie, I bet. Everybody wants to be in a movie. You do this, and people will watch you all over the world. Singapore and Argentina and Morocco. You know where Morocco is, kid?"

"No."

"Like a bull in a bullring," the uncle said. "Most bulls just get taken to the slaughter house and get killed with the cows. A bull in a bullring has some pain for an hour, but at least he gets to expose himself, show he has some character, you know what I mean? Think of it like that, Indian. Think of yourself as a bull in a bullring."

Rafael was looking at the heavy, square wooden chair. At the end of each arm, and at the foot of each leg was a thick leather strap.

"Yeah, the chair," the uncle said. "It looks authentic because it is authentic. Got it from the state pen back when the goody-goodies stopped electrocutions. Some real men have died in that chair. Lot's of 'em."

In the powerful light, Rafael saw dried blood in the cracks of the wooden chair.

"You ever seen a snuff film, Rafael?"

"No."

"One takes place in an operatin' room?"

"No."

"That was one of ours. Did well. Another one takes place in a cave?"

"No."

"Some people don't like 'em. Don't like to see how real men can take it. Tough guys like you, right, Rafael?" The uncle put his hand on Rafael's shoulder. "Get in the chair."

Barefooted, Rafael stepped over some thick, black cable on the floor. He turned around and sat in the chair.

"I want to explain to you exactly what will happen. What did Freedo tell you?"

"Not much," Rafael said. "Snuff film. Twenty-five thousand dollars."

"He must have told you something. I mean, described you. . ."

"A little," Rafael said. "I've got the idea. I understand."

"It probably won't even last an hour," the uncle said. "Just keep your mind on that. The time. It will be over. Eventually we will put you out of your pain. I expect you'll be glad when it finally happens."

"Yes," Rafael said. ". . .I 'spect so."

"I mean," the uncle said. "Look at the money."

"Yes."

"How else could a kid like you ever get so much money? Tell me that. Chance to show what you've got. What a man you are."

"This is against the law, isn't it?" Rafael asked. "I mean, movies like this."

"No," the uncle said. "Perfectly legal."

"I mean, makin' movies like this."

"Well, sure. Freedo told you . . ."

"Yeah."

"Now I want to explain everything to you, Rafael, see how you react, before we sign that contract, you see?"

"Yes."

"Two big, tough guys, giants, will bring you into camera range." The uncle swept his arm around the lit area to indicate camera range. "We use two cameras, one stationary—" he pointed to the central tripod—"and one handheld. We'll be filming you with two cameras at once, Rafael. Only one cameraman. He'll set the stationary camera and then move around with the other camera, taking close-ups, shooting you from all kinds of different angles. You'll forget he's there, after a while. It's better if you don't look at the cameras, I mean, straight into them. Make like they aren't there."

"Okay."

"Anyway, these two big guys will drag you in. Fight 'em as much as you want, I mean, really struggle with 'em. Do anything you know how to do, to get away from 'em. You can't hurt 'em. These guys used to be professional wrestlers. No matter what you do, you won't be able to get away from 'em? See what I mean?"

"Yes."

"By then you'll probably be fightin' in earnest anyway. I've seen even the toughest guys change their minds once things get rollin', when they get right up to it. Fight like hell. Make it interestin'. That's what we call in films makin' the action interestin'."

"Okay."

"There'll be a big, rough lookin' club over here, leanin' against a table. On the table will be the pliers, the knives and like that, gleamin' in the light. I don't need to tell ya, when you first see 'em and remember what they're gonna be used for, you'll be hollerin' and fightin' to get out of here, believe me. I've seen the toughest guys shit themselves right then and there. It's okay if you do. It's natural, I mean."

"Okay."

"I mean, the thing to think about this, Rafael, is that it's real. This isn't like other movies you've seen. We're not playin' around with ketchup and visual effects. We're really doin' what it looks like we're doin'."

"I know. Freedo—"

"So if you feel like shittin' your pants, or tryin' to bite one of these guys, you're welcome."

Sitting back, Rafael put his forearms flat on the arms of the chair. "Okay."

"Remember those apes will be enjoyin' it more 'n you are. Those guys are really nuts. I mean, like they like to give pain. They live for it. Okay. While you're wrazzlin' around, they'll get your clothes off you. Give 'em as hard a time as you can, you understand what I mean?"

"Yes."

"You an Indian? Probably we'll rig some kind of a breech cloth on you, you know, fancy jock strap, arms bands, leg bands, maybe put a little war paint on your cheek bones. That's what I'm thinkin' now. Make this one a little different. It'll sell better. We'll give this one some kind of a fancy title. 'The Brave' is what I'm thinkin' of at the minute. You like that? It just came into my head. This is a creative business. I'm a filmmaker. You mind if we do that? I mean, dress you that way before we start with this?"

Rafael did not know what he minded.

"War paint on your cheekbones will make your eyes stand out more, for the camera. 'The Brave.' Pretty cool. And you're a cool kid, Rafael. People will see this film all over the world, you know. How does that make you feel? 'Some kind of brave,' they'll say. About you."

"Even if I shit myself?"

"Jesus. This is authentic, Rafael. Real. Everyone will know what's happenin' to you. Who wouldn't shit himself? In snuff films, Rafael, don't worry: even the audience shits itself. That's the point, man: this is real."

The powerful light on Rafael, what the uncle was saying, were making Rafael light-headed.

"Now I want you to know exactly what's goin' to happen, how I've scripted this one. Okay?"

"Okay."

"I mean, before we make any deal between us, work up that contract."

"Okay."

"They'll get your clothes, rip your breech cloth

off you, tear off your armbands, leg bands, whatever we work up, and strap you into the chair."
The uncle pointed at Rafael where he sat and
smiled. He moved his arm to point at where he said
the table would be. "Your arms and your legs. This
is where the filmin' begins to get a little difficult.
While one guy is standin' over you in the chair, the
other will come over to the table and slowly choose
an instrument."

"What does that mean? I'm only askin'."

"He'll pick up a big, shiny, new pair of pliers,
work it in his fingers a little, know what I mean?
They're both real monsters."

"Pliers?"

"Then he'll slowly come over to you with the
pliers and pull out one of your fingernails. Don't
cut your nails between now and then, okay? Make
it easier for him to grab onto one. Your arms will be
strapped to the chair. Your legs will be, too. Make a
fist of your hand if you want. Don't worry. He'll
pry it open."

In the chair, Rafael made a fist of his right hand,
looked at it.

"Then one guy will force open your jaw—don't
worry, we know how to do that—and the guy with
the pliers probably will put a foot against your
chest and yank out a couple of your front teeth."

A radio in the outer office was turned on. Rafael
heard dance music.

"Enough to make blood come from your mouth. The other guy will be makin' wild gestures as if he's tryin' to stop you from screamin'. That's his act, you see. The screamin' is botherin' him. He puts his hands over his ears, cuffs you around the head . . ."

"I'm not supposed to be screamin'? You don't want me screamin'?"

"Sure! Scream all you like. Not to worry: you'll be screamin' all right. Who could help it?"

"Oh."

"It's all right to scream, Rafael. So the other guy will be over at the table. . ."—the uncle gestured again toward where the table would be—". . .pickin' out and tryin' a shears."

"What's a shears?"

"Big scissors."

"Oh."

"He'll kneel in front of you and clip off one of your toes. Probably a big toe. So then we'll have you bleedin' from both the head and the foot."

"One foot?"

"Good idea. Maybe both feet. The big toe from each foot. The other guy's real bothered by your screamin'."

In the outer office, the phone rang.

"So it will go this way," the uncle said. "I want you to understand everything, Rafael."

The radio was turned down. Rafael could hear the nephew talking on the telephone.

"He'll take a sharp knife and cut along here." The uncle ran the back of his finger along the top of Rafael's left thigh. "Both legs. Deep enough to get the blood pourin'. And up here." Gently, he ran his finger down Rafael's left bicep. "Both arms. And then here." With the ball of his index finger, the uncle indicated curved lines over both of Rafael's breasts.

"Why won't I bleed to death?"

"Won't be time. Just remember, Rafael: you're a tough guy; you're showin' what a man you are here, willin' to have all this happen to you; the pain will be over. Just remember, sooner or later, the pain will be over. You'll be out of your misery. But at this point, you'll be screamin', lookin' down at all the blood pourin' out of you, your eyes buggin' out of your head." The fat uncle took a deep breath, smiled and shook his head. "The audience just loves blood, lots of blood."

Rafael's mouth was dry. He put the side of his index finger into his mouth and bit down on it. He caused himself a little pain.

"Then the guy will get a spoon from the table."

Rafael cleared his throat. "A spoon?"

The uncle waved his hand in front of Rafael's face. "Both your eyes good?"

"Sure."

"One better than the other?"

"I don't think so."

"'Cause it's important as to where we place the club, you see." Always a director, the fat uncle waved his arms to Rafael's left and his right. "He's gonna spoon out one of your eyeballs and leave it danglin' on your cheek. We want the club to be on the side your remainin' eye is on, because about now, believe me, you'll be lookin' for that club. The audience will think you're lookin' at it with the ultimate terror. Actually you'll be lookin' for it for the ultimate relief. See, that's called irony. There always has to be irony in a film. You don't understand these things, Rafael, but I do. I'm a filmmaker. What we're makin' here maybe are the most important films ever bein' made because they're real, Rafael, none of this pretend stuff, we're showin' how real people take real pain and death, and there's art in them, irony, Rafael, and you're gonna be in one of these films, show what a man you are." The uncle took a deep breath. "So we'll spoon out whichever eye is the one away from the club. You see how everything has to be thought out in advance?"

Rafael swallowed drily.

"Then he'll get spear-like things, but with shorter staffs, arrows, but with thicker points, and he'll force them in here and here." The uncle pressed his finger into the two points at the top of Rafael's chest just inside his shoulders.

"The other guy will still be whappin' you on the

head, tryin' to get you to stop screamin'. He gets
his point across to the other monster, who returns
to the table, gets another pair of shears, returns to
you. While one holds your jaw open again, the guy
with the shears pulls out your tongue and snips it
off."

Rafael was holding his right hand against the
base of his stomach. "Supposing . . ." he said.

"Sure, Rafael. Ask me anything."

"Supposing, I mean, on the day we do this,
supposing on the day we do this, I puke all over
myself?"

"That's good, Rafael. You're really thinkin',
now. Try, if you can, to hit the guys with your
puke, you see what I mean, puke on them. It will
give them something more to react to, make them
pretend rage, justify what they're doin' to you,
you see what I mean? I mean, of course you'll
puke. Eat a big breakfast."

Rafael was breathing hard.

He was shivering.

Looking down, he saw in that bright light his
whole body covered with sweat.

"You okay, kid?"

The radio was louder now. Rafael heard a few
words of a weather report. "Sure."

"I mean, if you'd rather not know what's gonna
happen. . ."

"I'm okay."

The uncle turned away from Rafael. "Then he gets a little hand saw, spreads your legs wide and cuts it off."

"What?" He stared at the back of the fat man's white shirt. "I didn't hear you."

The man turned around. He pointed into Rafael's crotch. "Cuts if off."

Rafael looked down at himself. His penis engorged with blood.

The uncle smiled. "That's right. That's good. You won't be needin' it no more, Rafael. You know that. It's part of the movie."

Wave after wave of violent shaking went through Rafael's body.

"You'll still have one eye. . ."

As he closed his eyes, in that bright light Rafael saw the face of the fat man with the bulging eyes, smiling.

"While one of the guys is holding up what he's cut off for the audience to see, the other will unstrap one of your arms. You won't have much fight in you at this point, kid. You might still try to get out of the chair, I dunno. He'll go get a real sharp knife and cut your stomach out, you see what I mean?" Gently, the uncle drew and line in a half circle just under Rafael's rib cage. "And drop it in your lap. Maybe he'll dig some of your guts out with his hands. Your free hand probably will fight him, be down there in the mess of your own guts, too."

Eyes closed, Rafael was hearing the fat man's voice as if from far away. Behind the man's voice he heard the dance music from the radio.

"The other one will come up behind you with the club and smash open your skull. It will all be over for you then, Rafael. He's real good at it. Don't worry. I've seen him do it before. Very quick. One blow and your head's a broken mess, brains all over yourself. I've never seen him fail. You won't feel a thing."

For a moment Rafael sat in the square wooden chair, eyes closed, breathing slowly, deeply through his nose, the waves of shaking passing over his body.

"You okay, kid?"

Suddenly Rafael knew that the fat uncle had had pleasure from describing all this to him, that this had been part of it. He had earned some of the money already.

"Yeah."

Rafael felt the man's fat hand on his sweaty shoulder, then on the back of his neck. He opened his eyes.

"Come on. Stand up."

Bracing Rafael with his hand at the back of Rafael's neck, the uncle helped Rafael to his feet.

"So what do you think, kid?"

Rafael's legs, knees were rubbery. He stretched one arm to the back of the chair and braced himself.

"I think," Rafael said: "Thirty thousand dollars."

The uncle laughed. "Jeez, you're a tough guy! You drive a hard bargain all right. What a tough guy! You'll do. Okay. I give. Thirty thousand dollars it is." He shook Rafael's hand. "We gotta deal."

d

"LARRY, COME in here."

While the nephew stood in the office doorway, inside the office Rafael put on his clothes and the uncle poured vodka into the two used cups and talked.

"I've never seen a braver one than this one, Larry. One brave Indian hombre, I tell you. Tough as they come. . ."

Leaning against the door jam, Larry watched Rafael dress and said nothing.

"Drove a hell of a hard bargain, too. We have to give this kid thirty thousand dollars. Would you believe that?"

Larry said nothing.

"It will make a great movie, though." The uncle swallowed the vodka in one of the cups and poured himself another. "One of the greatest. Be seen all over the world, won't it, kid? Just like I told you. It will be seen all over the world, won't it, Larry?"

Larry said nothing.

The uncle handed the other cup of vodka over

the desk to Rafael. "Think of that. A kid from Morgantown in a movie seen all over the world."

Rafael threw the drink down his throat.

"Don't worry about Larry." The uncle put the top back on the bottle. "He's a dopehead."

Rafael put on his shirt.

"Now this is what I want you to do, Larry: take good care of this boy. We've got a contract, now, and it has to work just right. You know how I am about my contracts, Larry. Once I give my word, that's it. I want you to take this boy and open a bank account for him. You ever open a bank account, Rafael?"

"No."

"Larry will help you." When the fat uncle sat behind the desk the chair wheezed. He put his hands behind his head. Rafael saw the armpits of the man's white shirt were soaked. "Let's see now, what are we gonna do?" He looked at Rafael. "I mean, when do you want to do it, kid?"

"Today's Monday," Rafael said. "Friday?"

"Wednesday," the uncle said.

"I got a family."

"We can be set up by Wednesday."

Rafael shrugged. "I want to do things with my family."

"Sure. You want to get blind drunk," the uncle said.

"Maybe that too."

"Uh?"

"Maybe."

"Guess you have that right. Under the circumstances. Thursday. That will give you time to get drunk and set things up for your family."

"Thursday. . ." Rafael squinted at the high ceiling. "Okay."

"Be here ten o'clock in the morning."

"Eleven," Rafael said. "Don't want to take the early bus."

"Why not?"

"People on that bus have jobs."

The uncle laughed. "You have a job, Rafael."

Rafael grinned. "Yeah. Well."

"Okay. We'll make it eleven o'clock Thursday. Okay? Is eleven o'clock Thursday okay for you, Rafael?"

"Yes."

"Because you're the brave guy here doin' this thing and we want to make everything as nice as possible for you, you know what I mean?"

"Appreciate it," Rafael said.

"Okay. Eleven o'clock Thursday it is." The uncle lowered his arms onto his desk. "Now, Larry, take Rafael here to the barbershop, you know, the one over on Thirteenth, get him a haircut, not too short, we want him to look like an Indian boy here. Larry, I didn't tell you my great idea. We're gonna make Rafael here look even more

like an Indian, put him in a breech cloth, arm
bands, leg bands, a little war paint on his cheekbones, the whole bit. I think I'll call this film 'The
Brave' or 'How Brave' or somethin' like that. How
do you like that idea?"

Larry said nothing.

"So I don't want his hair short, you know what I
mean? But I want it neat, you know what I mean?
so he looks like a respectable, handsome Indian, not
a young street bum." The uncle grinned at Rafael.
"You get a handsome Indian and you get one real
handsome boy. Yes, sir. Walkin' in here you made
this our lucky day, Rafael. Right, Larry?"

Rafael smiled.

"Clean him up. Then take him to the bank. You
know which bank I mean. The bank we use our-
selves. The First Bank of Commerce. We know we
can trust that bank. Open an account for him. A
checking account. In his name. What are we gonna
give him up front? Two hundred and fifty dollars?"

On the piece of paper on the desk, the uncle
wrote $250.

"Three hundred," Rafael said.

"Oh, yeah." The uncle crossed out the $250 and
wrote $300. "Three hundred. In order to open a
bank account, Rafael, you have to put some money
into the bank. How much of the three hundred you
want to put in the bank?"

Rafael considered. "How much do I have to put in the bank to open an account?"

"Why don't you put fifty dollars in the bank, Rafael?" The uncle wrote $50 on the piece of paper on his desk. "That will give you $250 to take home with you, do what you want until Thursday morning." The uncle wrote $250 on the piece of paper.

"Okay."

"Be sure you give the checkbook to Rafael, Larry. It's to be in his name, see? Send him home with it. To his family. And he gets the two hundred and fifty dollars in cash. Fifty dollars in the bank."

Rafael asked, "What's the rest of it?"

"The rest of what?"

"The rest of the money? How does that happen?"

"Yeah," the uncle said. "First thing I do after you do your job Thursday is that I will personally go down to that bank myself and deposit the rest of the money for your family. Twenty nine thousand, seven hundred dollars." The uncle wrote $29,700.00 on the piece of paper.

Rafael's throat tightened. "How will I know. . . ?"

"You don't trust me, kid?" The uncle's face flushed. "How else we supposed to do it? You tell me that!"

"I don't know," Rafael said.

"We put thirty thousand dollars in the bank, think we'd ever see you again? You'd grab your family and run like hell." Rafael said nothing. "Nobody's ever ripped me off, boy."

Red-faced, Rafael said quietly, "I wouldn't rip you off."

The uncle grinned at Larry. "Well, I would. At least, I'd try. Tell me the truth, Rafael: that's what you were thinkin', weren't you?"

"No, sir."

"Try to get the thirty thousand dollars off me and grab your family and run."

"No, sir."

"That's called theft, Rafael. Robbery. You tryin' to rob me?"

"No, sir, I'm not."

"I wouldn't think so. Not a good, brave kid like you." The uncle smiled again. "You got any other idea how we can do it, Rafael?"

Rafael thought a moment. "No, sir."

"Because if you have, tell me right now and we'll discuss it."

"I haven't."

"You ever been paid in your life, Rafael, before you did a job?"

"No, sir."

"You ever even gotten an advance of money like I'm offerin' you before you did a job?"

"No."

The uncle loudly asked, "Then how in Christ's name you expect to be fully paid before doin' this job? Answer me that!"

Rafael said, "I don't know. I just want to make sure my family gets the money. My wife . . ."

"You don't trust me, Rafael?"

"Sure."

"Jeez, everybody trusts me. Don't they, Larry?" He glared at his nephew.

Larry said, "Sure."

"See? Larry works with me. He knows everybody trusts me. Shit, boy, I'm a business man. My word is as good as gold. It has to be. You think I could stay in this business long as I have if people didn't trust me?"

Rafael said nothing.

"We got a contract!" The uncle hit the paper on his desk with the back of his hand. "You think a contract means nothin', Rafael?"

"I don't know."

"Well, I'll tell you. A businessman does not oblige his contracts, he can be put in jail!" The uncle fixed Rafael in the eye. "In jail, Rafael."

Rafael said, "I see."

"For example," again the uncle put the back of his fingers on the piece of paper on his desk, "you sign this contract, accept the three hundred dollars, go off and get drunk, never come back, you know what we're gonna do?"

Rafael did not ask.

"We're gonna come look for you. We'll go out to Morgantown. If we can't find you, we'll show our contract to the law. One of your relatives, your wife, one of your brothers, your father, maybe, will have to give us the three hundred dollars back."

Rafael considered the sheer impossibility of that.

"Or go to jail," the uncle said. "For theft. For robbery." He pointed his finger at Rafael. "For your robbery."

Rafael swallowed through his tightened throat.

"You want that to happen, Rafael?"

Rafael shook his head.

Smiling again, the uncle said, "See, that's how it works. Never mind, kid. I know you haven't got much experience in business. I'm not insulted. You're a brave, tough kid, and you've made a hard bargain here, you sure have, but Larry and I know you haven't much experience in business. Never mind. Forget about it."

Rafael sighed.

Quietly, the uncle repeated, "After you do your job Thursday personally I will go down to that bank myself and deposit the rest of the money for your family." Again he wrote on the piece of paper, $29,700.00. "That's a lot of money."

"Okay."

"Think how happy your wife will be. You just

keep that in mind. That's why you came in here, isn't it? Isn't it, Rafael?"

"Yes."

"Okay." The uncle looked at Larry. "It's a done deal."

Rafael asked, "Where's the contract?"

"This is the contract." The uncle held up the piece of paper. "What do think I been writin'?"

On the piece of paper was written, Rafael, $250, crossed out, $300, $50, $250, and $29,700.00 twice.

The uncle studied it. "Standard. You ready to sign it, Rafael?" He put the paper flat on the desk and turned it around, facing Rafael. He tried to hand Rafael the pen.

Hands on the edge of the desk, leaning over the piece of paper, Rafael thought a moment. He said, "Put in about Thursday. Eleven o'clock Thursday."

The uncle laughed and turned the paper back toward himself. "Jeez, Larry! This kid doesn't miss a trick! I forgot to put in about Thursday eleven o'clock. Okay!" He wrote Thursday 11:AM on the paper and turned it back toward Rafael. "You were right not to sign it without that in it, kid."

Rafael took the pen. Slowly, carefully he wrote, R a e l.

Taking the paper, looking at it, the uncle said, "That's fine. That's just right, Rafael."

"Now you sign it," Rafael said.

"Sure. Of course. That's how contracts work. We both sign it. Mutual obligation." On the piece of paper the uncle wrote, Morocco. He showed it to Rafael. "There we are. All signed, sealed and delivered."

"Sealed?" Rafael asked.

"Just an expression. Forget the envelope." The uncle folded the piece of paper and handed it to Rafael. "You gonna leave this for your wife to find?"

Rafael stood with the folded contract in his hands. "I guess so."

"That and the checkbook from the bank Larry fixes up for you"

"Yeah."

"Then, you see, if that money isn't in the bank, your relatives can come after me." The uncle's eyes glinted into Rafael's.

Rafael said, "Damn' right."

Sitting back in his chair, the uncle put his hands behind his head again. "You're not gonna tell your wife, anyone, about this, are ya, kid? I mean, before?"

Rafael stared at the wall over the uncle's head.

Softly, the uncle said, "It would ruin your last days together. You can see that."

Rafael said, "Yes."

"Sure, they'd see how brave you are and all, and

be grateful plenty to you, but, you know, kid, they'd just be sad, too, and troubled. You want to enjoy your last days together with your family, don't you, in Morgantown?"

"Yes."

"Sure. You don't want a bunch of tears, everybody cryin'. Just leave the contract, the checkbook some place your wife can find it. Somebody will figure out what it all means and go get the money. Your father, maybe, or your brother that owns the truck."

"Yeah," Rafael said.

"That's the best way." The uncle stood up and put his arm across the desk to shake hands with Rafael. "You're a brave tough, smart kid, Rafael. You'll do fine. I have no doubts about that."

Rafael put his hand in the uncle's. The uncle held firm.

"Listen, Rafael. Thursday, eleven o'clock, you come here, we'll have a few drinks together. Get your courage up, okay?"

"Okay."

"I mean, you show up here too drunk, we'll just have to wait, and work you over, and that takes time and time costs money. You know what I mean? I mean, everybody will be here, the cameraman, the other two guys . . . See what I mean?"

With his hand still held by the uncle, Rafael said, "Yes."

"I understand you wantin' a drink and all. I'll give you drinks. When you get here. As much as you want. You hear what I'm sayin'?"

"Yes."

"What I mean, Rafael, is that if you show up too drunk and not lookin' good and we have to take the time to straighten you out, that costs money, and what we'll do is just take that money away from the twenty nine thousand, seven hundred dollars I expect to put in the bank for you. Your family will get less. You do understand that?"

Rafael said, "Yes."

The uncle gave Rafael's hand one firm shake and dropped it. "Take this rich kid to the bank, Larry," he said.

Larry said, "I need the money."

"Oh, yeah." The uncle took out his wallet and counted out six fifty dollar bills and handed them to his nephew.

Larry took the money. He said, "Haircut."

The uncle handed Larry another ten.

e

"CHEE! NOT in here!"

Immediately Rafael opened the door of Curly's Barbershop on Thirteenth Street the short, white-coated, mustached barber came forward with the palm of his hand up to stop him.

"No, you don't! Not in here, I said!"

He looked over Rafael's shoulder at Larry.

Rafael had stopped in the doorway.

His hand in the small of Rafael's back, Larry pushed him forward a few steps.

The barber backed up.

Larry closed the door.

"No!" the barber's face reddened. "I don't want him in here!"

"That's tough," Larry said. "You're gonna cut his hair."

"Never!" The barber closed his eyes and lowered his face.

Larry stepped around Rafael, and stood close to the barber. He looked down at the bald spot on the top of the barber's bent head. "Don't give me any your shit, okay?"

The barber's head snapped up. "You get him out of my barbershop, or I'm callin' the cops."

Larry smiled. "You happen to know a Mister Tony Fallon?"

The barber's eyes searched Larry's.

Larry said, "Mister Tony Fallon wouldn't like to hear you threw me out of your barbershop."

Hands on his waist, the barber looked at Rafael, at his hair. "This is impossible. I can't do it."

Larry pikced up a magazine and sat in a chair. "You'll do it."

"I won't touch him until he washes his hair. His whole head."

Larry said, "Don't bother me."

"I won't wash his hair."

Larry concentrated on the magazine.

The barber sighed. He said to Rafael, "Chee. There's a sink back here. You know how to use a sink, boy?"

At the back of the barbershop, the barber ran moderately warm water into a cracked sink. "God knows what diseases you've got."

"I'm healthy," Rafael said.

"Sure," the barber said. "'Healthy.' Drunk. Filthy."

Rafael looked down at his dusty jeans, cracked boots.

The barber handed him a plastic bottle. "This is shampoo. You know how to use shampoo?"

Holding it, Rafael studied the bottle as if he were reading the words on it.

"Put your head in the sink, soak your hair. Squeeze some of this soap from the bottle onto your head, lather it in, I mean, rub it around in your hair so there's soap everywhere, then stick your head in the sink again and rinse out, wash out all the soap." The barber held up two fingers. "Then do it again. You understand me?"

"Usually I use bar soap," Rafael explained.

"Well, this is called shampoo, and it's what you're gonna use now. Chee!"

The barber returned to the customer he had in his chair. The barber said to his customer, "I didn't touch him."

Rafael took off his shirt and dropped it on the floor. He lowered his head into the sink and used both hands to wet his hair thoroughly.

He heard the barber shouting. Straightening his back, he banged the back of his head against one of the water taps.

The barber, scissors in hand, had returned to the back of the shop and was red-faced. "Put your shirt on!"

Rafael looked at the water pouring down from his head onto his shoulders, chest, stomach. The top of his jeans were getting wet.

"Chee! Who told you to take off your shirt?"

"I'll get it wet!"

"So get it wet! Where do you think you are, anyway? Put on your shirt!"

Water in his eyes, Rafael found the shirt on the floor. He tried to shake the hair from the floor of the barbershop off his shirt.

The barber said, "Damned shirt's probably never been washed anyway."

"It's been washed," Rafael said. "Plenty."

The shirt hanging from his fingers, Rafael looked around the shop, at Larry concentrating on his magazine, at the middle-aged customer sitting in the barber chair watching Rafael through the mirror. "What's the matter with you, anyway, man?"

"There's nothing the matter with me!" The barber pointed the scissors at his own chest. "Look at how dirty you are."

"I'm not dirty," Rafael said. "My skin isn't dirty." He rubbed the ball of his thumb against his chest. "Sweaty, maybe. I've been sweatin'."

The barber glanced over his shoulder at Larry. He said quietly to Rafael, "Boy, you stink."

"I've been sweatin' a lot."

The barber took a step closer to Rafael. Still speaking quietly, he said, "I can smell your liver rotting."

Rafael stared down into the barber's face.

"Put your shirt on." The barber turned away. "Wash your hair."

Waving his scissors in the air, the barber returned to his customer.

At the back of the shop, Rafael still held his shirt
in his hand. He said, "I'm in the movies!"

"Sure you are!" the barber said.

"I am!"

"And I'm the president's wife!"

The customer in the barber chair laughed.

"Ask that man, that Larry there! He'll tell
you I'm in the movies. Aren't I in the movies,
Larry? Tell him I got a contract to be in the
movies."

Larry shifted in his chair. "Hurry up."

Rafael put his shirt on. He did not button it. He
washed his hair.

Dripping, he sat in the barber chair as soon as the
other customer left it.

Paying the barber, the customer said, "Good
luck."

"You come back, you hear?" The barber gave
the customer his change.

The customer pocketed the change. "I don't
know."

"Chee." Looking at Rafael in the chair, the
barber sighed. "Button your shirt."

"Button your shirt, Rafael," Larry said. "You're
makin' the little man excited."

The barber raised one finger to Larry.

"Listen close, shit," Larry said to the barber. "We want his hair cut right. Don't cut it short."

"I'd like to shave it," the barber said. "God knows what's been growin' in there."

"Cut it neat but long," Larry said. "Over his ears. Bring out his Indian look."

"'Indian.'"

"You do it right," Larry said, "or before we leave here, your head will be shaved as clean as a baby's ass. You got me?" Larry held out his right hand and showed how it could shake. "And I'm none too steady myself this morning." He raised his index finger to the barber. "No games. No tricks."

"Chee."

Larry returned to his magazine. He said, "He's in the movies."

The barber held up strands of Rafael's hair. "This mess ever been cut before?"

"Plenty," Rafael said. "My wife cuts it."

"What does she use, Chief, a hacksaw?"

"Sometimes I've cut it myself. It's been cut plenty of times."

"Ever been to a barber before, in your life?"

Rafael never had known what going to a barber for a haircut cost. "I like it the way my wife cuts it," he said.

"If she ever needs a job," the barber said, "send her to the guy down the street."

Rafael had never seen such a big, well-lit mirror before, surely never sat in front of one before, with almost nowhere else to look. The mirrors behind some of the bars at which he had sat had always been dark and pretty well covered by bottles of liquor and decayed signs for one brand or another. First he looked at the long fluorescent lights on the ceiling of the barbershop reflected in the mirror. He looked at Larry, behind him, sitting somewhat sideways in a chair, concentrating on his magazine. He looked at the other chairs along the wall, with metal tubular legs and arms. Most of the plastic-covered cushions on the arms of the chairs were ripped. Rafael thought of the big, square wooden chair he had sat naked in that morning, the dried blood in the cracks of the wood, the leather straps at the ends of the chair arms and legs. *Some real men have died in that chair*, the uncle had said. So would Rafael. He noticed himself smiling in the mirror. He had just realized he now knew something he had never known before, something very few people ever knew about themselves: where, and when, and how. . . he was going to die; in that chair, in that loft, Thursday, a little before noon. . . The barber, acting so superior, knew no such thing about himself, nor did Larry, the fat, fair kid so proud he could read, not even the uncle himself.

Rafael had been sitting in the barber chair several moments before he looked at himself in the mirror.

There was a cracked mirror in the bathroom of the trailer he used when he shaved a few times a week, but Rafael was not all that familiar with his looks. He noticed little pimples on his chin. For the most part his skin was smooth and dark. He had no beard lines, as many men have. His brothers also had very sparse body and facial hair. The skin around his eyes was his whitest, and, puffiest. His eyes were red-rimmed and bloodshot. There was the mark on Rafael's right jaw he had received the week before when he fell down drunk and hit his jaw against he did not know what. At least he thought that was what happened. He hoped no one had hit him on the jaw. Rafael noticed how thin his shoulders were. He was pretty sure his shoulders once had been heavier, more muscled than now. And his thighs, beneath his denim jeans were thin, but they always had been.

The short barber was concentrating on cutting Rafael's hair. He did not seem to be having such a bad time.

The barber had said he could smell Rafael's rotting liver.

Rafael wondered if that was true.

He wondered exactly what it meant about his liver.

About himself, it meant that as he was living, the life he was in, Rafael had no future. Somehow (and, it was true, Rafael did not exactly remember how) he had a wife and three children and they needed things, food, clothes to go to school, the trailer's propane gas tank filled so Rita could make warm meals, a few nice things, presents, toys so they would know they were loved, so many things he had seen and seen and seen over time he could not attain. The man from the government had stopped coming to Morgantown and then the checks from the government had stopped coming and then the food stamps had stopped. There had not been a delivery of the surplus food, the dried, old cheese, to Morgantown for a long time now. Some people explained the disappearance of the man and the money one way, others another way. Some said the government man was living very well in a suburb off the money that was supposed to come to Morgantown; they had seen him driving a new car. Others said he died. And still others said they had heard someone had decided to get rid of Morgantown altogether, the people there, by starving them out. Rafael's family, all the people in Morgantown, needed money to make their own lives go, they needed food more than they needed anybody. They needed money just to go, to leave Morgantown, to find places to live, jobs, to get to some place else, a place from which the government agent, money, food stamps, surplus food had not disappeared. Rafael did not know the answers to any of these questions; he had never thought he had known what he, his family ought do. To Rafael it seemed life had just happened to them. His response, no worse than most others, had been to try to drown the hunger, the pain, to stave it off, be as insensitive, insensate to it as possible, ignore it as the best means of surviving it. Rafael had some understanding of how sick he was. He guessed he could smell his own liver rotting. As a young man, he knew he was as helplessly drunk as some of the oldest men in Morgantown. He had seen them dead of rotted livers, dehydrated dead in the August sun, frozen dead on the December earth. The uncle had said, *A year from now I probably even wouldn't want ya. You'll be totally worthless.* Rafael knew that was about right. The uncle had said, *I think you're right to be doin' what you're doin'.*

It had taken him weeks to figure out, ever since Freedo first spoke to him about the job, but Rafael did figure that he had only one thing to sell for money, and that was time.

The uncle had said, *You can stand an hour of anything, isn't that right?*

Better an hour, Rafael reasoned, than a year.

Better to cash in a year, or two . . .

"Finished with the movie star." The barber dropped his scissors and comb into his wash basin. "Hope I never see him again."

Standing up, Larry said, "You never will."

With his hands, Rafael tried brushing his cut hair off the front of his wet shirt. He had noticed the barber had covered the front of his earlier customer with a cloth, but had not spread a cloth on him.

"Take your shit outside, Chief," the barber said.

Larry's hand was on the doorknob.

"Hey!" the barber said sharply.

"Suck it," Larry said. "You're swallowin' this one."

"What the hell?" the barber asked.

"You expect me to pay you?" Larry asked. "After all the shit you gave me?"

"God damn!"

"Jerk off." Larry opened the door. "Come on, movie star."

f

"WHY?" WALKING
down the busy noontime city street with him, several times Larry had glanced sideways at Rafael.
"Why so what?" Rafael said.
"So why are you takin' on this job?" Larry asked.
Rafael giggled. "Why not?"
Taking him by the elbow, Larry steered Rafael around a group of well-dressed people outside a restaurant. Larry had set a fast walking pace. "Not much future in it."
"Haven't got much future anyway," Rafael said.
"Didn't you hear what Mister McCarthy said?"
"Who's Mister McCarthy?"
"Your uncle."
"No. What does he know?"
"I'm a drunk," Rafael said.
Again Larry cut his eyes at Rafael. "You're young. Younger'n I am."
"That makes it worse."
"You like to drink," Larry said, "stay alive to drink."
"Not enough money," Rafael said. "Not ever enough to drink."

"You mean, to kill yourself?"

Rafael stumbled stepping off a curb. "Worth more dead than alive," Rafael said. "I heard a man on television say that about himself. That's me. I'm worth more dead than alive."

"I don't get why you're doin' it this way."

"Got a family." The hot sun, the fast walking pace, the air, the confusion of all the people on the sidewalk was making Rafael feel more drunk than he had felt sitting in the barber chair. "It's all over for me, bozo."

"Why don't you do it quick and quiet then?"

"Do what?"

"Get it over with. Make it easy on yourself."

"Naw," Rafael said. "That wouldn't do anybody any good."

"It's your flesh and blood, I guess," Larry said. "Wait here a minute."

Leaving Rafael in the hot sun at the edge of the sidewalk, Larry approached three young men huddled near the corner of the building. One wore an ankle length horse coat and a hat with a very wide brim.

Larry shook hands with each of the three but really only spoke to the one in the long coat.

After a short conversation, Larry took the wad of fifty dollar bills his uncle had given him out of his pocket. He peeled off one fifty dollar bill. To the fifty he added the ten dollar bill his uncle had given him for Rafael's haircut. He handed both bills to the man.

The youngest man, standing to the right of the long-coated man, took plastiscene bags out of his pocket, counted out a few, and handed them to Larry. The long coated man checked the number of the bags.

Larry put the bags into his pocket.

Without saying anything more, Larry resumed walking down the sidewalk at his quick pace.

He nodded to Rafael to join him.

Catching up to him, Rafael said, "You do drugs."

"So?"

"You're no better'n I am," Rafael said. "You'll come to it."

"Come to what?"

"You know."

"Never," Larry said. "You might try really good shit, you know. Before you go. Might change your mind about things. You owe it to yourself to try it."

Rafael smiled. "That shit'll kill ya."

After they turned the corner onto Commercial Street, Rafael chuckled. "I'm keepin' you in shit, I guess."

After going through two sets of glass doors, Rafael found himself in a huge, high ceilinged room. The room was more cold than cool. The floor and the walls were of smooth, white stone. The furniture, the teller booths, the desks at which people sat, taller desks in the middle of the floor at which people stood, the railings were of dark, polished wood.

All the people in the room were well dressed. Most of the men wore jackets and neck ties. One woman at a desk wore an open sweater over her blouse.

Most of the people were looking at Rafael standing inside the door gawking.

Larry said to the woman at the desk nearest the door, "This boy needs to open a checking account."

"Oh, yes." Her eyes scanning Rafael said she doubted that was what Rafael needed. "I'll ask Miss Christie to help you."

"Who's Miss Christie?" Larry looked over the rows of desks one side of the room.

"The woman in pink and black." The receptionist was picking up the telephone to call only a meter or two.

"Come on," Larry said to Rafael.

By the time they got to Miss Christie's desk she had answered the phone. Her eyebrows rose as she looked at Larry and Rafael.

Larry lifted a side chair from the next desk and sat down beside Miss Christie's desk.

"I see," Miss Christie said into the telephone. She hung up.

Larry said, "He's opening a checking account."

"Is he?" Miss Christie spoke as if needed permission had not been granted.

"What's your full name, Rafael?" Larry asked.

"Brown."

"Rafael Brown," Larry said to Miss Christie.

Slowly, Miss Christie withdrew a single sheet of paper, a printed form, from a desk drawer. "How much will you be depositing initially into the account?"

Larry peeled another bill from the bunch his uncle had given him and put it on the desk. "Fifty dollars."

"Is that enough?" Rafael smiled at Miss Christie.

Larry said, "Shut up, Rafael."

"Is that with a ph or an f?" Miss Christie asked.

"Is what?" Larry asked.

"Rafael," she stated.

Larry waited for Rafael to answer. Larry finally answered, "Make it with an f."

Pen poised over her paper, Miss Christie asked, "Doesn't he know?"

"F is right," Rafael said.

"Address?" Miss Christie asked.

"Morgantown," Rafael answered.

"Street address?"

"There are no streets," Rafael answered. "Not really."

"Is Morgantown a real place?" Miss Christie asked.

Larry laughed. "You ever seen it?"

Miss Christie said, "I've heard about it. I doubt there's a post office there."

"People leave things at the store," Rafael said. "The little store. That's where all the mail to Morgantown goes."

"From what I've heard Morgantown is due to be plowed under." Miss Christie sighed. "Does 'the little store' have a name?"

"The store," Rafael said. "Everybody just calls it the store."

Writing, Miss Christie said, "'The Store, Morgantown.' Social security number?"

Rafael said, "340J96728S."

"My, my," Larry said. "You have applied for jobs."

"Sure," Rafael said. "All the time."

"Next of kin?" Miss Christie asked.

"Closest living relative," Larry said.

"Rita."

"Rita Brown," Larry said.

"Is she your mother or your wife?" Miss Christie asked.

"Wife," said Rafael.

"I was afraid you'd say that." Miss Christie sighed. "And I suppose you produce children."

"Three."

"Will this be a joint checking account? I mean,

do you want your wife to be able to make deposits
and withdrawals, write checks on it, too?"

"Never mind," Larry said.

"Yes," said Rafael. "Withdrawals."

"Very well. Besides the check book I will give
you, I will also send you home with a signature
card, a card for your wife to sign. She must sign it
and you must bring the card back to the bank before
she can write any checks. Do you understand that?"

Rafael said, "Just right."

"If you'll just give me a moment to enter all
this. . ." Miss Christie turned to her keyboard.

While Miss Christie worked, Rafael remained
standing in front of the desk. He looked around the
bank. No one was looking at him any more.

Larry was fingering the plastiscene bags in his
pocket.

"Now I need your signature," Miss Christie said.

Carefully, Rafael wrote R a f e l.

"That's your signature?" Miss Christie asked.

"That's how I write my name."

"Where's your last name? I don't see your last
name."

"Oh." Rafael leaned over the desk again. He
wrote B r o o n.

Miss Christie said, "Oh, dear." She picked the
fifty dollar bill up off her desk and walked across
the room with it and her papers.

Rafael held out his hand, palm up, to Larry. "Give me the rest of my money."

"Oh. Yeah." Larry reached into his other pocket, drew out the mess of fifty dollar bills, and put the mess on Rafael's palm.

Holding the money in the open palm of his hand, Rafael said, "There's one missing."

"Did you count it?" Larry asked.

"Larry, I know there's one missing."

"How many are there supposed to be?" Larry took the mess of bills out of Rafael's palm. "There are supposed to be four, Rafael."

"I know you gave one to the guy for drugs, Larry."

Slowly, Larry counted the bills out on the edge of Miss Christie's desk. "One, two, three, four. There are supposed to be four." Larry handed the bills more neatly arranged back to Rafael. "And there are four. Just like I said."

Rafael looked at the bills in his hand. "Where's the other fifty, Larry?"

"You gave it to the woman."

"What woman?"

"She's depositing it in your bank account, Rafael. You put it in the bank. That's how it works, remember?"

Rafael was fingering the bills one by one when Miss Christie returned.

"This is your temporary checkbook, Mister

'Broon'," she said. "And this is the signature card for your wife to fill out and sign. Do you know how to write a check?"

"Doesn't need to." Larry stood up.

Miss Christie smiled at Larry. "It should be all right," she said, "if his Social Security number is accurate."

In his hands, Rafael held the checkbook, the signature card, and two hundred dollars in cash. His contract was in the back pocket of his jeans.

"If you need help, maybe your friend can show you how to write checks and keep your stubs in order."

Larry was walking toward the glass doors of the bank to the street.

"Larry!" Rafael shouted.

He hurried after Larry. Everyone in the bank was looking at him again.

He stopped Larry on the sidewalk.

In the bright sunlight, Rafael smiled. "Will you be there Thursday?"

"Not me," Larry said.

At his quick pace, Larry walked along the busy sidewalk back the way they had come.

Rafael watched Larry until he turned the corner onto Thirteenth Street.

g

RAFAEL PULLED a shopping cart free from the long line just inside the entrance of the store.

It was a huge store. Rafael had had to cross an enormous parking lot to get to it.

He had been in this store before, but never with so much money in his pocket.

He had thought he would stop for a couple of drinks before he came to this big store, so he could think about things, the shopping he was about to do, enjoy his thinking. Frankie was much too young for a baseball glove, of course, not yet one year old, but Rafael thought that maybe if Frankie had a baseball glove left him by his father, maybe he would play the game, be accepted on a team somewhere other than Morgantown, get into the world somehow, maybe even become a great player, recognized as a person far and wide. Marta, nearly two years old, always was humming some little song she had heard somewhere or of her own creation. Rafael wanted to buy her some sort of a musical instrument. Lina, at two and a half, would put sticks in rag beds with rocks as their pillows

67

and say 'good night' to them. But Rafael did not want to buy Lina a doll. There were enough babies to mother. He thought he wanted to buy her something bigger, more encouraging than a doll. From the sticks she was making her own dolls, even giving the sticks names.

He was a stranger in the tavern he found. The bartender asked to see his money before he brought him a neat vodka. The other people in the tavern all looked to Rafael like they had jobs, or could get jobs, although they were lined up at the bar drinking in the early afternoon. Rafael thought it must be nice to have a job and also be able to drink in the afternoon. Well, he had a job, too. A job that started Thursday. And ended Thursday. And he could afford a drink in the afternoon, too. He was uncomfortable in that tavern. The other people lined up at the bar probably thought they were better because they had jobs that let them stop by for a drink in the afternoon but they really were not better because they did not know the essential thing about themselves: where and when and how they were going to die. Rafael only had the one drink and left.

In the big store he steered the shopping cart toward the circular racks of women's dresses.

"Hey," Rafael said to a girl also shopping. "Would this dress fit you?"

He held up a blue and white dress he liked. He

had also found a red and black dress he thought
would look good on Rita.

The girl smiled at him. "You buyin' me a dress?"

"No. For someone about your size."

"What exact size is she? I mean, a size six?"

"I don't know. About as tall as you. Only skin-
nier."

"Skinny like you?"

"Yeah. I guess."

"Your girl friend?"

"My wife."

"Oh. Try size six. If she's skinny like you
maybe you ought to think of buyin' one with a
belt."

"Oh." The blue and white dress did not have a
belt on it. The red and black dress had a cloth tie.
He put the blue and white back on the rack and
held up the red and black. "How do you tell it's
size six?"

"You look at the label." She stood close to him to
find the label inside the dress's neck. "See? Size six."

"Oh. Okay." Quickly he grabbed a blue and
yellow dress off the rack. It had a plastic belt. "Is
this a size six?"

The girl looked at the label. "Yes." Standing
back, her eyes smiling, she asked, "Which one you
gonna buy?"

"Both of 'em." Rafael dumped the dresses into
the shopping cart. "I got plenty money."

Rafael wandered around the huge store with his shopping cart until he came across the toy section.

In an aisle empty of people he came across an electronic keyboard instrument. It looked like those he had seen on television, only smaller.

He put his finger on one of the keys. A startling, loud, clear sound came out of the machine.

He put his finger on another key. The sound lasted as long as he depressed the key.

A teen-aged boy in black pants, white shirt and black bow tie, appeared at the end of the aisle. "You gonna buy that thing?"

"Hey," Rafael said. "You got a job here?"

"I work here. Yes."

"This thing make music?"

The boy approached. "If you know how."

Rafael stood back. "Make me some music."

The boy spread his hands over the keys.

Rafael recognized the first notes of *Amazing Grace*. "Wow!"

"It can do all sorts of things." The boy flipped a switch, depressed another key, and another sound altogether came out of the machine.

"I want that." Rafael began to pick it up to put it in his shopping cart.

"No!" The boy grabbed Rafael's arm. "It's plugged in! This is a demonstrator model. You have to buy from stock."

Narrowing his eyes, Rafael asked, "Is that the same thing?"

"Sure." The boy lifted a box from underneath the counter. He showed the picture on the sealed box to Rafael. "Same thing."

Rafael compared the picture on the box to the wonderful machine on the counter. "It looks the same."

"It is the same," the boy said. "You want it?"

"How much does it cost?"

The boy smoothed the price sticker with his thumb. "Thirty nine fifty."

"Okay." Rafael took the box from the boy. The box was a little too long for the shopping cart so he put it in the basket with one end sticking up. "Hey. You know where boxing mitts are?"

"Boxing mitts?"

"I mean, baseball gloves. Baseball mitts."

"Sure. Over here. Sports."

Pushing his cart, Rafael followed the boy down the aisle. As they were going along a wider corridor, a picture on another box caught Rafael's eye. "Hey! What's this?"

The boy turned back to look. "That's a play doctor set."

"What does that do?"

The boy picked up the box and held it so they both could see the picture. "Kids can play doctor with it. See? There's a stethoscope, tongue depressors, 'unbreakable thermometer', it says, headlamp, I guess. I don't know what that thing is. It all comes with a little black bag."

"Doctor," Rafael said. "Cool. That cost much?"

The boy looked into Rafael's eyes. "It says twenty seven ninety five."

Rafael took it from him and put it in his shopping cart.

"You still want a baseball glove?"

"Yeah."

"What position?" The boy led Rafael into another aisle.

Rafael answered. "For the hand."

"Right hand, left hand?"

"I don't know yet."

"For yourself?"

"My kid."

The boy grinned. "Still a baby?"

"Yeah."

There was a big display of baseball gloves on the counter. A chain ran through them locked to the counter.

"So what position do you want your kid to play? Catcher?"

"Not a catcher."

"First base? Outfield? Pitcher?"

"Pitcher," Rafael said.

The boy pointed out the right glove. "I guess you want a boy's size."

"Yeah. Do I have to buy that from stock?"

Again the boy dived under the counter. He came up with the box with the appropriate picture.

"Thanks." Rafael put that box in his shopping cart.

"We all done?" the boy asked.

"Point me to the food counters."

"That way." The boy waved behind him. "My name is Kent."

"Mine is Rafael."

"I mean," Kent said, "while you're waiting in the checkout line you might fill out a form saying I was helpful. We each try to be Employee of the Month. It depends on how many slips we get made out on us." Again he looked into Rafael's eyes. "Never mind."

Rafael repeated: "Thanks."

He pushed his cart along a wide aisle, came to shelves of canned food, boxes of cereal, turned his cart and strolled along the glassed meat section. He stopped when he saw the frozen chickens. There seemed to be more kinds of chicken there than he had ever noticed before.

A woman dressed in white came along the back of the counter. "May I help you?"

"You have a turkey?" Once, in that store, Rafael

and Rita had seen a turkey. Rita said she had never seen one before. They studied it through the glass until someone came along behind the counter to help them or shoo them off. Of course they had not the money for a turkey. Neither had ever had turkey.

"You want a turkey?" the woman asked.

"I think so. How much they cost?"

"Sixty nine cents a pound. I can give you a nice, tender bird, twenty three pounds."

Sixty nine cents a pound! Maybe they could have afforded one before.

"I'll take it."

The woman returned from the freezer and handed a twenty three pound frozen turkey over the counter to Rafael.

Rafael put the frozen bird in his shopping cart.

Looking at his shopping cart, at all these things in it, the big, frozen turkey, the baseball glove box, the play doctor box, the musical instrument box sticking out of the basket, at the bottom of everything two dresses, one red and black, the other blue and yellow, Rafael laughed.

Behind the counter, the woman laughed, too. "Come back," she said.

Pushing his shopping cart toward the check out counters at the main entrance, Rafael found himself going through the men's clothing section. He slowed.

There was no point in buying anything for himself. Was there? He looked down at this thin, faded shirt. His jeans were greasy and torn. His boots cracked. He stopped. He pictured himself getting off the bus with all his bundles on the road above Morgantown in fresh, bright clothes. It would be nice to have the people, Rita, at least Lina, maybe even Marta remember him that way rather than in the hand-me-downs and rags he had always worn, that he was wearing right then.

The woman who worked in that section said to him from some distance away, "Really big sale goin' on. Jeans twelve dollars. Shirts eight dollars."

Twelve dollars. . . eight dollars. . . Shoot, he must have that much money left.

"Can I try 'em on?" Rafael asked her.

"Sure." She pointed toward a door with a mirror on it.

Rafael found some jeans and a bright red and white checked shirt he thought would fit him.

He left the door to the changing booth open a crack so he could keep his eye on his shopping cart outside.

The jeans were a little loose and a little long but with his belt they rode on his hips well enough. The shirt was scratchy on his skin but smelled nice. He rolled up his sleeves.

He wanted to wear these clothes home.

He transferred his cash, checkbook, contract, an

old cigarette lighter he had found and a few toothpicks he had taken from some tavern from the
pockets of his old jeans to his new. His old clothes
were sprawled on the floor of the dressing booth.
He did not want them any more. After considering
leaving them where they were he realized he did
not want anyone to see them anymore, have to deal
with them, worry that perhaps someone had forgotten them, left them there by mistake. He rolled
his old shirt and jeans in a ball and stuck them
under the dressing booth's bench.

Outside the booth he looked at himself in the
full-length mirror on the door. With his hair
washed and trimmed, his new shirt, new jeans,
Rafael thought he looked much happier. To his
own eyes he looked quite different from the young
man who had sat dripping wet and dirty in the
barber chair only two hours before. For a moment
he wondered what he was doing, what he had
agreed to do, what had happened to him to make
such a change in his appearance. Surely his new
appearance, seeing him this way, would make his
family happy.

And surely there was no reason at all for him to
spend money on new boots.

A gray-haired, well-dressed woman also pushing a shopping cart followed him in the check-out
line.

Fingering the tags on his shirt and jeans, Rafael

said to the check-out woman, "I've left the tags on
these clothes so you can charge me for them."

Behind thick lenses, the check-out woman's eyes
were hard. She reached behind the counter.

Rafael thought he saw her press a button. She
was probably counting the customers or something.

He took the turkey, the boxes, the dresses out of
the cart and placed them on the counter while she
rang them up.

"My clothes," he said.

Two men appeared beside him.

One nodded at the tags on his clothes. "Come
with us," he said.

"Where?"

The man took Rafael by the elbow.

"My things," Rafael said. "My shopping."

"Leave them there."

The man let go of Rafael's elbow but still walked
beside him. The other man walked right behind
Rafael. They went through the store and into a
small office in back.

"I've got to catch a bus," Rafael said. "The
three-thirty bus."

"You're goin' to jail," one of the men said.

"Me? Why?"

"What do you call takin' things from a store
without payin' for 'em?"

"What?"

The man flicked the tags on Rafael's shirt and jeans with his fingernail. "'What,'" the man repeated. "You're a smart one. Didn't even rip off the tags."

"I wouldn't rip you off," Rafael said.

"Probably doesn't even know about the electronic devices on the clothes," the other one said.

"Real smart."

"I was goin' to pay for them," Rafael said. "That's why I left the tags on."

"Sure," the first man said. "You were tryin' to wear clothes you haven't paid for out of the store."

"I want to wear the clothes home. On the bus."

"Sure," the man said. "Where are your old clothes?"

The second man asked, "Are you drunk?"

"Maybe a little." Rafael wiped his dry lips with the back of his hand.

One man said to another, "I can smell it. The booze."

The other man asked Rafael, "You actin' this stupid because you're drunk?"

"Stupid?" Rafael asked.

"Come on." One of the men held out his hand. "Turn out your pockets."

Rafael was glad to remember he had put his contract, folded, flat in one of his back pockets.

With pride, he handed the man his cash, and, his

check book. Also he handed him his cigarette
lighter and toothpicks.

The other man felt Rafael's back pockets. "No
wallet."

"No identification?"

"I don't use a wallet." Rafael didn't have a
wallet. He had nothing to put in a wallet.

"Driver's license?" the man asked.

"He has almost two hundred dollars here."

"To pay for the things I was buying."

"Fifty dollars in this checking account. Depos-
ited today."

Rafael said, "That fuckin' Larry."

"Watch your fuckin' mouth, boy."

"No cigarettes. Guess we know what this lighter
is for." The man flicked it several times. "It doesn't
work."

"How much was your bill out there, Indian?"

"I don't know. The woman hadn't finished
ringin' it up."

"How much had she rung up?"

"I don't know."

"More'n two hundred dollars worth?"

"Where are your old clothes?"

Rafael blushed. "I left them in the booth."

"Let's go see about that."

The men escorted Rafael through the store again
to the mens' department. Again, everyone was
looking closely at Rafael.

Rafael pointed. "That room."

One man opened wide the booth's door. "They're not here."

Softly, Rafael said, "Under the bench."

"What?"

"Under the bench. I stuffed them under the bench."

The man bent over and pulled the bunched shirt and jeans from under the bench. "Jeez! Filthy!" His face said he wanted to be sick at the sight, the feel of them.

"That's why I left them there."

The man holding the clothes said, "Where you spend your time, boy?"

The other man called to the saleswoman in the men's department, "Ms. Willikins, get a bag and dispose of these things."

"You left your clothes here," the man holding Rafael's clothes in one hand said, "so you could sneak the clothes you're wearing, you were steal-ing, through check-out without being noticed. Isn't that right?"

"No. I was gonna pay for 'em."

"Pretty stupid."

"You stop callin' me that," Rafael said.

"What, 'stupid?'"

"Tha's right." Suddenly, Rafael wished he had had two drinks in that tavern. Maybe three. He wished he had not come into this store. His happy thoughts had dried up, were dry in his mouth.

Ms. Willikins appeared with a paper bag. She held the top open.

The man dropped Rafael's old clothes into the bag. "Throw that in the garbage," he said.

"He's not a vagrant," said the other man. "He has money. A checkbook."

"Let's go back to the office." Again the man took Rafael's elbow. "Call the cops."

"No," Rafael said. "I have to be on that bus. Today I have to go home. With my presents."

Again the two men walked Rafael through the store, everybody staring at him.

"The three-thirty bus," Rafael said.

Inside the office waited the gray-haired, well-dressed woman who had been behind Rafael in the check-out line. Her purchases in paper bags were on a chair.

"Yes, ma'am?" One of the men asked.

Rafael's money and checkbook and lighter and toothpicks were still on the desk.

Speaking more clearly than Rafael had ever heard anyone not on radio or television speak, the woman said, "I was behind this young man in line at the check out counter. Immediately he said to the cashier, 'I've left the tags on these clothes so you can charge me for them.' Again, while she was ringing up his other purchases, he reminded her to charge him for his clothes. She should never have summoned you."

"You two know each other?" The man looked from Rafael to the woman and back again.

The woman said, "I beg your pardon?"

"I guess not," the man muttered.

The woman picked up her bundles. "That's all I have to say."

As she was going through the door, Rafael said to her, "Thank you, ma'am."

Looking back at Rafael, she said, "Fair's fair."

One of the men scratched the back of his head. "Okay. Let's go see how much over two hundred and whatever dollars your bill is."

Rafael put his money, his checkbook, his lighter and toothpicks back into his pockets.

Going through the huge store again, the men walked a little further away from Rafael, a little slower.

The turkey, boxes, dresses were back in the shopping cart.

"How much was his bill so far, Susan?" one of the men asked the cashier.

Reading from a slip, the hard-eyed cashier said, "One twenty six eighty two."

"That include tax?"

"Yes."

"Include the shirt and jeans."

The cashier stepped close to Rafael and read the tags hanging from his shirt and jeans and rang up twelve dollars and eight dollars and the tax. She added that sum to the sum on the slip on the counter. "One forty seven sixty two," she said.

Rafael pulled out his money and handed all of it to the woman.

"You makin' off with anythin' else?" One of the men tried to pull up Rafael's pants legs to look at his socks.

"Leave me alone," Rafael said.

The cashier said, "This is too much money."

The other man said, "This guy's just stupid."

The cashier handed Rafael back some money then rang up the sale and handed him back more money.

Rafael stuffed the money in his pocket.

Looking at the cart, Rafael realized there was too much in it for him to carry. He also saw that none of it had been put in bags.

Ignoring the men, he pushed the shopping cart through the door to the parking lot.

The men followed him outside.

"Hey, kid!" one of the men shouted.

With his loaded shopping cart in the sunlight, Rafael stopped and looked back at the men.

"We know your face. We'll be watching for you. Don't you ever come back to this store again."

Rafael smiled radiantly at the men. "As a matter of actual fact," he said. "I won't."

h

RAFAEL PUSHED his loaded shopping cart into Freedo's tavern.

A bartender shouted at him: "Don't bring that thing in here!"

"What else am I gonna do with it?" Rafael asked. "Can't leave it outside."

"Outside, you!" the bartender said.

Leaning against the far end of the bar, Freedo said, "That's all right."

"What?" the bartender asked.

"Leave him be," Freedo said.

Rafael wheeled his shopping cart to the bar. He sat on a stool. "Give me a beer," he said to the bartender. "I thirst."

Rafael had supposed the two men in the huge store thought Rafael was using the shopping cart to bring his purchases out to a car or truck in the parking lot. Waiting for his beer, he smiled. So who was stupid? He had said he didn't have a driver's license. He had said he was taking the three-thirty bus. He couldn't possibly carry all that bulky stuff, the baseball glove box, the play doctor box, the musical instrument box, two dresses and a frozen twenty three pound turkey to a bus stop by himself. While the two men stood at the door watching him, Rafael zigzagged through the parking lot with his shopping cart. After they re-entered the store, he trundled his shopping cart down the sidewalk several blocks to Freedo's tavern near the bus stop.

He swallowed most of his cold beer.

From where he leaned against the darkest section of the bar, Freedo was staring at Rafael. Even in the dark, Freedo's eyes glinted.

After a moment, after Rafael had finished his beer, Freedo picked up a shot glass and a bottle of vodka as he came up the bar. He put the shot glass in front of Rafael and filled it with vodka.

"I didn't ask for that," Rafael said.

"On the house."

Freedo never had bought him a drink before.

"How come?" Rafael asked.

"Don't you want it?"

"Truth is, I'm real thirsty," Rafael said.

Without saying anything, Freedo put a fresh beer on the bar in front of Rafael.

"Truth is," Rafael said, "I could do with a glass of water."

Freedo put ice in a tall glass, poured water from the tap into the glass, and set it on the bar in front of Rafael.

"Thanks."

Freedo nodded to the shopping cart next to Rafael. "Spent some money."

"Yeah." Rafael drank the water. "For my wife and kids."

"Got a new shirt, too, haven't ya?"

"Yeah. Feels funny." Rafael wriggled his shoulders. "Crinkly, you know?" He laughed.

Eyes still glinting weirdly, Freedo asked, "You done what I think you done, Rafaelo?"

"Maybe." Rafael drank the vodka.

"Jesus." Freedo shook his head and looked at the floor.

"It will be okay," Rafael said.

"Jesus H. Christ."

"Listen," Rafael said.

Freedo listened.

Rafael said, "It will be okay."

"'Okay,'" Freedo repeated.

"It will."

"Sure," said Freedo. "It will get over, I guess. I mean, sooner or later, it will be over."

"That's life," Rafael said. "It will get over. One way or the other, sooner or later it will be over."

"So now you've got some money."

On his barstool, Rafael straightened his back. "Made a good deal."

"Don't tell me about it."

"That Mister McCarthy's all right. I could deal with him."

"Who?"

"He added something to the contract, you know? I asked him for . . . So they can't find fault with me, keep people waitin', charge me for it, until the bus gets in."

"Contract?"

"But that nephew of his, Larry, phew!"

"You met Larry."

"Son of a bitch stiffed me for fifty bucks."

"Son of a bitch."

"Helpin' me set up the bank account, for Rita."

"I see."

"Guess I should thank you, Freedo, for tellin' me about this."

"I never thought you'd do this, Rafael. Actually do it. Shit!"

"Come on." Rafael grinned. "I'm gonna be in the movies. Seen all over the world, Mister McCarthy said. Like a bull. I'm gonna go out like a bull. I'm like a bull in a bullring, Mister McCarthy said."

"You ever seen a snuff movie, Rafael?"

Rafael smiled. "Never been in a movie theater."

Freedo filled the shot glass with vodka. "Did Mister McCarthy tell you what's gonna happen to you?"

"Yeah."

"In detail?"

"He told me everything. He's got a real electric chair. He said, 'Real men have died in that chair.'"

"I'm sure."

"Sure," Rafael said. "What time is it?"

"Mean to catch the three-thirty bus today, Rafael?"

"Yeah."

"You've got a few minutes yet."

Rafael drank the vodka. His eyes became wet. "What else can I do?"

"I dunno." Freedo examined his chipped fingernail. "I guess people do this. I mean, what you're gonna do. These films exist. People have done it before."

"You seen 'em? You ever seen a snuff film, Freedo?"

"Yes."

"The point is, they're real," Rafael said.

"I know."

"Not like the other movies. They're just pretend."

"Jesus."

The other bartender said, "That turkey's drippin' all over the floor."

"It's all right," Freedo said.

"Well, I'm not gonna clean it up."

Freedo shouted: "I said, it's all right!"

The bartender looked at Rafael. "Suddenly you got a pet drunk?"

"So when are you gonna do this?" Freedo asked Rafael.

"Thursday."

"Jesus H. Christ."

"Yeah. Got a couple of days."

Freedo said, "And you got some money."

Rafael hesitated. "Yeah."

Freedo walked up the bar, picked up a bar rag, and walked back.

"Way to go, Rafaelo," Freedo said.

"Sorry about the water on the floor," Rafael said. "The turkey water."

"Forget about it."

"Must be about time for the bus." Rafael finished his second beer.

"Wait a minute." Freedo slid open a cupboard door behind the bar. He took out a fresh half-gallon bottle of vodka. He lifted it over the bar to Rafael. "Put this in your cart."

"What're you doin'?"

"Take it."

"I never owned one of those before."

"It'll go with the turkey."

"What're you doin'?" the other bartender asked.

"I can't hold this here all day," Freedo said. "Take it."

The other bartender said, "That's illegal!"

"Well, thanks." Rafael took the bottle and put it in his shopping cart.

"Hey!" the other bartender said.

Freedo said to the bartender, "This is my bar. That's my vodka."

"And that's your pet drunk, I guess!" the bartender said.

"Shut the fuck up!"

"You'll kill him!"

"That's not funny," Freedo said.

"I wanted to be funny, I'd work in a delicatessen," the bartender said.

"Just shut up. It's almost three thirty, Rafael."

"What, he has to get home from school on time?" the bartender asked.

Standing, Rafael reached his hand over the bar.

After looking into Rafael's face a moment, Freedo shook hands with him.

The bartender said, "Good riddance!"

Freedo said, "Way to go."

i

COMING OFF the bus, instantly Rafael felt and then saw Rita's eyes fixed on him.

Hands on her hips, the children around her feet, she stood outside the travel trailer which was their home looking up the side of the gully at him to the highway where the bus had stopped. Her head tilted slightly sideways.

Rafael knew that even at that distance, Rita was seeing there was something different about him.

Rafael put some of his packages on the dirt at the side of the road. He had to return to the bus for the dresses, turkey and half-gallon bottle of vodka.

Of course the bus driver had not permitted Rafael to put the shopping cart aboard the bus. Rafael abandoned the cart on the sidewalk at the bus stop. Whimsically he wondered if the huge store which had given him such a hard time would ever get its shopping cart back.

Coming through the town nearest Morgantown, a real town called Big Dry Lake with supermarkets and banks and fast food places, the bus slowed to work its way around three police cars parked in the

driving lanes of the road outside the big liquor
store. Two policemen stood on the sidewalk talking to people. Through the bus window and the
window of the store, Rafael could see more uniformed policemen in the liquor store. Outside the
store other people stood around, shoppers and
merchants, a couple of boys holding bicycles, gos-
siping.

Rafael guessed the liquor store had been robbed.

To his own surprise, on the bus ride from the
city to Morgantown, Rafael had not taken a drink.
He had not unscrewed the cap of the half-gallon
bottle of vodka Freedo had given him. He had not
wanted a drink. Usually on the bus ride home,
lowering his head behind the back of the seat in
front of him, filling his mouth, then tossing his
head back, he would finish a pint. He supposed he
could do the same thing, though not as easily, with
the half-gallon bottle. He saw this big bottle not so
much as a container of liquor as some sort of
trophy. He was eager to get to Morgantown, to
arrive in fresh clothes, to give Rita her dresses, see
her face, give Lina, Marta and Frankie their presents. Then maybe he would drink.

The second time Rafael came off the bus he saw
Rita climbing the side of the gully to him. Lina was
following her.

As the bus roared off, swirling dust, Rafael
waited for her.

Feet separated in the dust, arms reaching to the sky, Rafael stretched.

An illegal, unplanned-for, not engineered dirt road, unwanted by the authorities, led down from the highway halfway up the rise into the gully that was Morgantown. Pulling out of that dirt road at a reverse angle to the traffic was dangerous. Even putting the gas pedal to the floorboard could not get any vehicle up to the speed of the traffic flow. Over the years, several people had died trying, or had died or been hurt because someone else had tried. It was the only access road to Morgantown. Many times the authorities had tried blocking it off, first with a wooden barrier, then with metal guard rails, finally with big boulders. Always the impediments had been moved by the people of Morgantown.

Morgantown was not a real town. Originally there had been a cement-block gas station, general store there with considerable acreage owned by an old man named Morgan. He was still alive when Rafael was a child. Originally the gas station-store had serviced a two-lane road. A few trailers, owned and rented out by Morgan, settled around the store. The old man himself, and his wife, while she lived, resided in a double-wide trailer behind the store. Electricity and water ran from the store to all these trailers.

Rafael remembered something of the excitement

when he was a child as the new highway was being
built, approaching day by day from Big Dry Lake.
To everyone's amazement, as the highway approached it moved away from the gas station-store.
It began to rise into the air and be cut into the side
of the high hillside. As the men worked on the
highway, they dropped earth and boulders and
beer cans onto Morgantown. No access to the gas
station-store was deemed safe; none was planned;
none was built.

Some time before he died Morgan sold off the
hundreds of acres behind the gas station-store.

That dry land was turned into a dump.

A limited-access ramp was arranged off the highway in the flats a quarter mile from Morgantown.
An unpaved road led from the ramp through the
main gate of the dump. A chain-link fence surrounding the dump now ran for miles. One section
of the fence ran twenty meters behind the store.
Old Morgan's double-wide almost backed onto it.
Day by day by day for years now trucks of all
kinds, pick-ups, dump trucks, even tankers had
pulled off the highway, shifted along the unpaved
road into the dump. If the weather was dry, as
usual, each truck raised an enormous cloud of dust.
Together the trucks dumped probably every kind
of refuse under the sun into that dump.

Just as the barriers the authorities built across the
road from the highway down to Morgantown did

not keep the people in, the chain-link fence around the dump did not keep the people out.

Holes were cut in the fence. The men, the women, the children of Morgantown scavenged the dump for anything they could turn into cash money.

Although sometimes someone might get a few days of real work, at a real job, the dump was the main source of cash money for the people of Morgantown.

When Morgan died, no one knew who owned the gas station-store. No one seemed to care. The cement block building remained. When Rafael's brother's truck, or the other, bigger truck brought scrap metal into the junk yard in Big Dry Lake, it returned with boxes of cereal, sometimes fresh fruits and vegetables, baloney, hamburger, milk, beer, vodka, cigarettes and whatever cash money remained to be dispersed to the people who had collected the scrap metal from the dump and loaded the truck that time. The foodstuffs would be put in the cement block building. It looked more like a warehouse than a store. People would take what they needed and put about the right amount of money, more or less, into the always open drawer of the cash register on the counter. That money, too, would be brought to town and used to purchase food the next trip. There was no accounting. Some people in Morgantown, like Mama, had no source of money and therefore could never put

money in the register but still had to eat. Occasion-
ally a few people, especially a few men who had
been thought to take more vodka and cigarettes
than they had contributed to the register, had to be
spoken to, urged, even dragged along on scavenge
trips to make up the difference. For the most part,
this imprecise economy worked without much
acrimony.

After Morgan died, no one ever had come along
to put the people off this land, to claim it as his
own. After a while, the electricity was turned off.
No one had ever received a bill. Always before
they had paid what they owed to Morgan. Unsuc-
cessful efforts were made to collect the money to
pay the electricity bill and to have electricity
turned on again. Never enough money was collected to satisfy the bill and the electric company
had no patience with these people. So the gas
pumps and the water pumps no longer worked.

From that point forward, the gas station-store
was just "the store."

"Morgantown" was the name the people in Big
Dry Lake and its environs gave the gully. The
people in the gully seldom referred to the place as
such. Morgan had died a long time before. They
had a cemetery in the gully and sometimes the
Roman Catholic priest from Big Dry Lake
dropped by to see them but the people in the gully
knew they weren't a town.

People around there also referred to the people living in the gully as "homeless". Sometimes drifters showed up hitch-hiking or in cars that could not go another mile, or could not make it up the hillside highway, and some of these stayed until they found a way to go. Some stayed until they died.

The people in the gully did not consider themselves homeless. Three families lived in what was left of Morgan's double wide. Other combinations of people lived in the other trailers or in vans which sat on the earth flat on their wheels. There were plenty of abandoned cars in the gully which could shelter a drifter for a night or a week. For example, Rafael and Rita, very young, moved into a single axle travel tailer which had been pulled into the gully by an old man one storming night. The old man had never gotten out of the car during the storm and no one had gone to see about him and once the storm was over, the next afternoon, he was found dead held up in the driver's seat by his seat belt. He was buried and his ancient car sold in parts. For another example, when it was noticed Mama smelled too awful to continue living where she was, a huge packing crate had been emptied and gotten over the dump fence somehow and set up for her near the store. Her big, soft bed with the brass bedstead was set up first, and a bedside table. The packing crate then was turned over to cover the bed and table. A door was cut in one corner

away from the bed. Over the bed a big window
was cut so Mama could sit up in the bed and see
everybody in the gully, watch the children play,
talk with people who came by. Heavy, sliding
curtains were arranged for both the bed and the
window. A cardboard picture with a small cut in it
of a lake among snow-capped mountains found in
the dump was nailed onto the wall facing her bed.
Stencils on four sides of the outside of the crate said
URBINE, UR INE, TURBINE and TUR INE.
Both Rafael and Rita, perhaps cousins, had been
born in that gully.

There were homes in the gully between the
highway and the dump.

Rita reached the soft shoulder of the highway.
Brushing her hair wet with sweat away from her
face, she looked at Rafael's purchases on the
ground, his new jeans and shirt. She looked into his
face.

She said, "What?"

Rafael smiled. He hugged her neck.

She stepped back. "You're not drunk."

"Not very."

"You're always drunk when you get off the
bus," she said. "What happened to your hair?"

"It was cut."

"Who cut it?"

Rafael made his fingers work like a scissors.
"Barbershop. I went to a barbershop."

"How much did that cost?"

He answered honestly, in a way. "Nothing."

Lina was still struggling up the slope from the gully.

"What are all these things?" Rita asked.

Rafael picked up the two dresses he had folded carefully over his other purchases on the ground.

"For you. You like them?"

Her fingers touched one dress and then the other. "Very. They have price tags on them."

"I bought them."

"How?"

"I have a job."

"Then why aren't you working at it?"

"Thursday," Rafael said. "I have to go back to the city Thursday."

"Rafael," Rita said. "They did not pay you for work you have not yet done."

"I did some work today," Rafael said. "It was very difficult."

"Doing what?"

"In a warehouse. The boss liked me. He paid me a lot because he wants me to come back Thursday."

Rita looked at all the things on the ground Rafael had brought with him and laughed. "A turkey?"

"Yes." Rafael laughed, too. "I bought a turkey."

"It's so big!"

Rafael handed his wife the dresses.

He crouched. As Lina toddled to him, he hugged her. "Lina, Lina, Lina." Then he said, "Look what I have for Lina!" He took the play doctor box and showed Lina the picture on it of the stethoscope, tongue depressors, unbreakable thermometer.

Lina looked closely at the small picture at a corner of the box of a boy with a stethoscope around his neck and a reflector on his forehead.

Still crouching, Rafael watched his wife holding the dresses against her body, admiring them. In the gully two or three people had stopped whatever they were doing to watch frankly Rafael and Rita and Lina beside the highway.

Rita smiled at him. Her eyes were wet. "You're crazy," she said.

"Come on." Standing up, leaning over, Rafael picked up the other two boxes, the turkey, the half-gallon bottle of vodka. He started down the slope.

Rita followed him, carrying the two dresses in her hand shoulder high, away from her body.

Halfway down the slope, Lina slipped and fell. Her chest landed on the play doctor box.

Rafael looked around at her. "Come on, Lina!"

The first person they met was Rafael's brother, Nito. Nito had a beer can in his hand and blood in his eyes. He focused on the vodka bottle dangling from one of Rafael's fingers. He said, "Herma-nito. . ."

Rafael laughed. "Later, Nito!"

A woman they passed, one who lived in the double wide, stood silently. Her eyes examined the dresses Rita was carrying.

Rafael's father sat in the shade of the store with another old man. They sat in bent, torn lawn chairs from the dump. Empty pint vodka bottles were at their feet. His father's eyes and cheeks were wet. His nose was running. He said, "My teeth, Rafael."

Rafael hesitated. "Maybe we'll get them fixed."

"Just to be rid of them, Rafael," his father said. "To have them out."

Rafael smiled. "I tell you: I'll do that."

"It's no good unless you can get out the roots," the other old man said. "It's the roots that hurt. Can you do that, Rafael? Can you take out the roots of your father's teeth?"

Rafael shrugged. "I don't know."

"Did you find work, Rafael?" The other old man ran his eyes over all the new things.

Rafael nodded. "In the city. I have to go back Thursday."

"How much they payin' you?"

"In a warehouse," Rafael said. "A special kind of warehouse."

"They have any more jobs to give out?"

"Not right now," Rafael said. "I asked."

While he was moving away, Rafael heard the old man notify Rafael's father, "Rafael's found work."

"Eh," Rafael's father said. "The young can do anything."

"Lina! What have you there?" In her packing crate, Mama was sitting up in her bed looking and calling through her window.

Lina held her box up as high as she could so Mama could see the pictures on the box.

"Did Lina get a present?"

Lina nodded energetically.

Walking backward in the dust, Rafael watched and listened to them. He should have brought Mama a present, too. He could have afforded a present for Rita's grandmother.

Outside his own trailer, Marta sat in the dust. Looking no higher than his knees, she watched her father approach. She hummed a little song.

Rafael put the baseball glove box, the turkey, the bottle of vodka on the floor just inside the opened door of the trailer.

Crouching, Rafael put the biggest box flat in the dust in front of Marta so she could see the picture.

Looking at the size of the box, then at the over-sized picture on the box, the little girl's eyes grew wide.

"Marta gets a present, too," Rafael said.

Looking over Rafael's shoulder, Rita asked "What is it?"

"It makes music," Rafael said. "You should hear it."

Rita laughed. "You're crazy," she said.

Marta put the fingers of one hand onto the edge of the box. Then she lifted her hand. She put her fingers onto the box again, fitting the tips of them to the keys of the keyboard. She raised her hand again, slowly, and refitted her fingers to different keys. Her finger tips left dust on the box.

Rafael laughed. He tousled Marta's hair with his fingers. Then he stood up.

He glanced at Rita. Never had he seen more light coming from her face.

Frankie was asleep on the rags built up in his orange crate in the place nearest the trailer where there was shade all day except for earliest light. The rags just under the mid-section of his naked body were stained with fresh urine and defecation and stank. The baby had a light frown. He seemed to be concentrating on his sleep.

Rafael balanced the smallest box on one corner of the crate nearest Frankie's feet.

"Is that a baseball glove?" Rita asked.

"Yes."

"No one 'round here plays baseball."

"Sure they do."

Smiling, Rita said, "You're crazy."

She went up the steps and into the trailer.

Picking up the turkey, Rafael followed her. Inside the trailer, he put the turkey into the empty, aluminum sink basin in the kitchenette.

"What am I supposed to do with that thing?" Rita asked.

"Cook it."

"How am I to cook it?"

"I don't know."

"Rafael, there's nothing big enough in this whole place to cook that thing."

"Give some of it out," Rafael said.

"We'll have to fry pieces of it," Rita said.

"I'm not sure."

Turning, he held her to him. He kissed her face. For a long moment, he kissed her mouth, deeply.

With the heel of her hand, she pushed against his shoulder. She freed her mouth from his. "Will you get me buckets of water?"

At the bottom of the gully along the chain link fence that surrounded the dump there was a sluggish creek that was the source of all the water for the people of that place, for their washing, their bathing, their cooking, their drinking.

"How many buckets?" he asked.

"Four."

Four buckets of water at that hour meant Rita planned to wash the children and herself earlier than usual.

"Want to go watch the sun set tonight?" Rafael asked.

Rita grinned. "Might."

Rafael let go of her. "I'll get six buckets."

Outside the trailer, holding an empty plastic pail in each hand, Rafael turned back, stopped and stood looking at the trailer a moment. Lina sat on the steps of the trailer, taking things out of the play doctor box, dropping most of them in the dust. Marta sat on the ground as she was before, humming, admiring her box. Rafael wondered if Marta thought the box itself and not its contents was her present. The box with the baseball glove had tipped. One corner of it stood in Frankie's orange crate crib. The baby was silent. Inside the trailer, Rita coughed. On the steps, Lina coughed and rubbed her nose and eyes. Marta sneezed. Rafael took a deep breath.

Being able to do things for his family filled his heart with love for them.

j

W HEN RAFAEL en-
tered, the people sitting around in the store fell
silent. Never before in his life had that happened.

Rafael said, "I'm buyin.'"

There was a stirring of feet. Still no one said
anything.

He put a five and two one dollar bills into the
open drawer of the register.

He had brought six buckets of water to the trailer,
filling the bottom of the aluminum shower stall, first
stoppering the drain with a small rubber mat. Kneeling on the floor, Rita would bathe the children in the
water at the bottom of the stall. Then, sitting in the
water, knees up to her chin, she would bathe herself.
She would leave the water in the stall for Rafael to
use. He poured another bucket of water into the
kitchenette sink, first removing the turkey to the
sideboard, and stoppering that drain.

While she was bathing the children, he walked to
the store.

The silence suggested to Rafael the people in the
store had been talking about him before he entered.
That made him feel important.

Buying them all beer made him feel important, too.

He handed out four cans of beer. Taking one himself, opening it, drinking some of it, he sat on an upturned metal crate. A six-pack collar with one beer left in it, plus the full six-pack he placed on the floor at his feet.

The others sat on sufficiently mended chairs, mostly lawn chairs, from the dump. Rafael's father sat in a torn, broken overstuffed brown chair. He appeared more sober than he had before. In shorts, the boy, Ninja, sat on a box he had placed atop another box. His dirt stained legs dangled.

With all the windows removed, the store was cooler and less dusty than the outside in the late afternoons.

With mock pleasure in her voice, Marie said, "You have a job, Rafael?" Years before, Marie had worked as a chambermaid at a motel this side of Big Dry Lake. She had walked to her job along the highway before dawn every morning and back in the heat of early afternoon. She had five small children then and no husband. Finally the alcohol she drank made going to work every morning impossible. Except at dump picking, she had not worked since.

Rafael nodded.

Nito asked, "What's this about working in a warehouse, Rafael?"

"A warehouse," Rafael said.

"What do they handle there?"

Rafael answered, "Film."

"Film? Is that heavy work?"

"Yes," Rafael said. "The heaviest."

"How did you hear about this job, Rafael?" his father asked.

"A bartender. In the city."

"You never mentioned it," his father said.

"There wasn't time," Rafael said. "I went right over."

"Someone hired you after you had been drinking?" Marie asked.

"And you say there are no other jobs there?" Nito asked.

"Not right now."

"No one ever hired me after I had been drinking," Marie said.

"The boss even gave me a drink," Rafael said. "He drinks himself."

His father asked, "What's this boss's name, Rafael?"

"McCarthy," Rafael said. "His nephew, Larry, helps him run the place."

"You say the warehouse handles film?" Nito asked.

"Yes. For the movies."

"Would that be much film?" Nito asked.

Rafael shrugged. "It's a big loft."

"The movies," Ninja said.

Alessandro's voice was loud. "You're telling us this boss paid you before you ever did work? He gave you a drink and paid you?"

Rafael sipped from his can of beer. "I did work today. It was very hard."

"How long did you work today?" Nito asked.

"Two, three hours."

"How much an hour?"

"The boss advanced me some money."

"How much an hour?"

Alessandro said, "The boss gave you a drink, you did two, three hours work, and he advanced you a lot of money. Show me such a boss!"

"Someone cut your hair," Marie said.

Rafael sipped his beer and nodded.

"In a barbershop?" Ninja asked.

"Yes."

"How much did that cost?" Ninja asked.

"I didn't pay for it."

"Who paid for it?" Alessandro demanded.

Rafael shrugged again. "I guess he did it as a favor for the boss."

"Some boss!" Alessandro shouted.

"Nice shirt." Marie turned her beer can upside down over her mouth.

Rafael's father was staring at Rafael with hard eyes.

"I guess the boss wants me to look nice," Rafael said.

Nito snickered. "To work in a warehouse."

"There is no such boss!" Alessandro said.

"I have to go back Thursday," Rafael said in a low voice. "Then I will have to earn the money."

He realized he was picking his fingernails. He remembered Mister McCarthy had told him not to cut his fingernails so the pliers could get a good, easy grip on them.

Rafael put his hands in his pockets.

"Don't bring home sickness," Rafael's father said.

Looking at Rafael, Alessandro said, "Father Stratton is coming tomorrow."

Marie scoffed. "Father Stratton is always coming tomorrow."

"He pulled his car over to me when I was walking along the highway and said he would come here tomorrow," Alessandro said. "We'll see."

Marie said, "I will not go thirsty again waiting for Father Stratton."

Rafael said, "I plan to go to the church, anyway."

"When?" his father asked.

"Soon," Rafael answered. "Very soon. Maybe tomorrow."

Rafael's father asked, "You have something to

confess?" When he smiled his teeth, yellow and brown, crooked and cracked, were visible.

Rafael shrugged.

"You can confess to me, Rafael." Alessandro laughed. "I will give you penance."

Rafael's father said, "They fixed the fence today."

Nito nodded. "They have named a new manager of the dump. I heard that."

"I saw him," Ninja said. "He carries a gun."

"Ninja. . ." Marie said.

"He carries two guns. A rifle and one in a holster on his hip." With his right hand formed as a pistol, the boy showed how the new manager's pistol hung from his hips. "A big pistol. Maybe a six-shooter."

"You're imagining," Alessandro said.

"No," Nito said. "I believe it's true."

"What is wrong with stealing from the dump?" Rafael's father asked simply. "What is wrong with taking things other people don't want and have thrown away?"

"They don't want us there, Papa," Nito said. "They don't want us in the dump."

"We cut their fence," Alessandro said.

"I heard they are afraid we might get hurt there," Nito said. "Die there. Sue them."

"Ah, yes," Rafael's father said. "They don't want us to get hurt there. So they shoot us there."

"They can shoot us for trespassing," Nito said.

"It's public property," Alessandro said. "Like a park."

"It has a fence," Nito said.

"So do parks," Alessandro said.

"They don't want us to live," Marie said.

"Have you really seen this man, Ninja?" Rafael's father asked. "This man carrying two guns?"

"Yes," Ninja answered. "He shouted at me."

Rafael's father smiled. "He didn't shoot you."

"He waved the rifle at me."

"The guns probably are for shooting the rats," Rafael's father said.

"The rats!" Nito said. "It would take all the ammunition in the world to shoot the rats around here."

"We are the rats," Marie said.

Rafael's father shrugged. "We will have to cut more holes in the fence. A nuisance."

Rafael had heard his brother's truck stop outside. "Luis has his truck working."

"It's been working all day," his father said. "Since noon, anyway."

"It needed a new carburetor," Ninja said.

Rafael said, "I know."

"It took how many weeks for Luis to get the money for a new carburetor?" Nito asked. "Three?"

"Five," Marie said.

Nito said, "Five."

"We will cut a new hole in the fence," Rafael's father said. "Luis can take our findings from the dump to town to sell."

As Luis entered the store, he blinked his eyes to adjust from the bright sunlight outside to the shade inside the store.

"Have a beer," Rafael said.

"I'm going to." Luis stood by the counter.

"I mean, have one of my beers." Rafael held up the six-pack collar with one beer left on it.

Luis' eyes had adjusted so he could see what Rafael held up. He also saw the full six-pack at Rafael's feet.

"You buyin' beer for everybody, Rafael?"

Rafael grinned.

"I could have another." Alessandro crouched and tore a beer can from the six-pack on the floor.

Marie held out her hand for one. Alessandro handed it to her, and tore off another.

Luis took the can of beer from Rafael's hand, popped it open, and drank half of it.

Crouching, not saying anything, Ninja took his second beer.

"*Hombrito!*" Luis said. "I am as dry as an old lady's—excuse me, Marie."

"I am not an old lady," Marie said sadly.

Luis drained his beer can and took another off the floor. "You are buying beer for everybody, Rafael?"

"Rafael's rich," Marie said. "He has a job."

"Beer for everybody," Alessandro said. "Presents for everybody."

"What do you mean?" Luis asked.

"Look at his new clothes," Marie said.

"His haircut," said Ninja.

"He bought all his children presents," Alessandro said.

"Two dresses for Rita," Marie added.

Nito said, "The biggest bottle of vodka."

"And a big, big chicken," Ninja said. "Store bought."

"Turkey," Rafael said.

"I'm not," the boy answered.

"Is this true, Rafael?" Luis asked.

"Someone gave me the vodka," Rafael said.

"Someone *gave* him the vodka." Marie smiled as if she had something sour in her throat. "Someone *gave* him a haircut."

"You had no money this morning." Luis straddled an old wooden kitchen chair backward. "That I know of."

"I got a job," Rafael told his brother.

"A job! Where? Doing what? In the city?"

"In a warehouse. Do I have to tell about all this again?"

"You would not mind telling about it," Alessandro snapped, "if you were telling the truth."

"So much money in one day," Luis said. "Did you steal something from the warehouse, Rafael?"

"Rafael needs to go to confession," Rafael's father said.

"He must have stolen something." Neatly, Marie flicked the ash from her filtered cigarette into her empty beer can.

Rafael spoke low. "I didn't steal anything." He was feeling a little angry at these people suggesting he stole something while drinking his beer.

He looked down at his new shirt and felt better.

"What did you steal, Rafael?" Luis' tone was friendly. "How did you get rid of it?"

Rafael swallowed some of his beer and said nothing.

Softly, Ninja said, "Rafael done stole something."

"You stole something from the warehouse?" Alessandro asked loudly. "And you think you can go back to that job Thursday?"

With jaw tight, Rafael answered, "I'll be there."

"You'll be arrested!" Alessandro shouted. "You wait and see!"

"Better not go back," Luis said.

Rafael thought of the contract in his pocket, the checkbook, the card from the bank Rita must sign. He thought of saying to his brothers and father, *If I don't go back, you all will be arrested*, but he did not say it. Instead he said, "I have to. That's the deal."

"You should go to confession to Father Stratton, Rafael," his father said.

"How much did you get for it?" Luis asked.

"Enough," his father said. "Did you find something to do with your truck, Luis?"

"I was talking to this man," Luis said. "He is rebuilding a store. I was talking to him about carting away the stuff he is taking out of the store, old wall board, rubble, when the robbery and shooting happened. After that, he told me to come back and maybe we will talk some more tomorrow."

"Robbery?" Alessandro asked.

Ninja said, "Shooting?"

"You don't know." Luis talked and acted like a *caballero*, a man who had a horse, in this case, a truck, and had been away and back again. Sitting backward on a repaired kitchen chair, he spoke to them from the height of the driver's seat of a pickup truck. "That big liquor store in Big Dry Lake, you know the one? this side of town, was held up. The young woman who works there was shot, they say, through her breast."

"Liquor store." Nito looked at Rafael.

"Was much taken?" Alessandro asked.

"Don't know. I suppose so. Money from the cash register."

"Did anyone see the robber?" Rafael's father asked.

"They say 'young male.' That's all."

Rafael said, "They always say, 'young male.'"

Marie said, "It always is, 'young male.'"

"The young woman is dead," Luis said. "Shot dead. I saw them lift her out of the store. Her head was covered. She's dead."

Reaching for his beer, Ninja tipped over his can. He caught it before much spilled.

It took Rafael a moment to realize no one was speaking.

He cleared his throat. "I saw it, too," he said. "The robbery. Many cops."

"How did you see it?" Nito asked.

"Through the bus window. The bus passed by, I guess, after the robbery. I saw many cops in the liquor store."

"Were you on the bus, Rafael?" his father asked.

"You know it."

"No," his father said. "I do not know it."

"You saw me get off the bus."

"No," his father said. "I did not."

Rafael finished drinking his beer.

"Shot through her breast," Ninja said.

Staring at the floor, Nito said, "Liquor store."

Rafael stood up and stretched. His body felt oddly fatigued. He felt his body relaxed after strain. His appearing naked before the fat uncle so long must have tired his body somehow. He wondered how that could be.

He picked up the remaining six-pack collar from the floor. One remaining can of beer dangled from it.

He saw all eyes in the store were on the remaining full can of beer.

"I brought home a big turkey," he said. "After Rita finds a way of cooking it, we'll give you each some."

"Do I want turkey?" Alessandro said. "No. I don't think so."

"All right," Rafael said.

He started to leave the store.

His father said, "Luis, if you get this job carting away rubbish from that store, maybe Nito and Rafael could help you."

"Maybe," Luis said.

"That would be good," said Nito.

"Rafael?" Luis asked. "You want to help?"

"No," Rafael said from the door. "I have a job."

k

"HEY, RAFAELO!"

Walking past the shipping crate in which Mama lived, Rafael had forgotten to turn and greet her in the window. The can of beer on the six-pack collar still hung from his hand.

"Hey, Mama."

Squinting through the sunlight, Rafael looked at the massive woman propped up in her bed looking through the little window.

"You're lookin' sharp this afternoon, Rafael."

He looked down at himself. "New shirt. New jeans."

"And new dresses for Rita."

Rafael stepped into the shade of the crate. He handed Mama the can of beer through the window. "The beer is warm."

"Who cares?" Mama had the beer can mouth hole popped open and to her lips in an instant. She did not remove the six-pack collar. After a long drink, she wiped her mouth with the back of her hand. "It's been a warm day."

"Of course," Rafael said.

"Hey, Rafael," Mama said. "The funniest thing.

This morning, you know little Tita, three years old, lives in Morgan's old double wide now? just wearing underpants tipped over in that puddle that was there by the Ford." Rafael looked at where the puddle had been near the rusted, collapsed chassis. Now there was gray, sun crusted dirt. "The water in the puddle must have stung her rashes. She tore off her underpants and began running around in a circle hollering. You know, Rafael, it is my responsibility to yell at the children. What else can I do? Sometimes I have to laugh. Along comes Rocky's two boys, how old are they, five and six? young Rock and Jazz, and what they they do? They pick up Tita's dirty, wet underpants and run in a circle after her until they catch her. They put her underpants back on her. She hollers some more and runs away from them. She's taking down her underpants as she runs. She trips and falls. The boys catch her again and while she is on the ground they try to put her underpants back on. She's kickin' her little legs. One foot catches the smaller boy right on the nose. It begins to bleed. Blood and all, he's still tryin' to get her pants back on her. I'm laughin' so hard, I can hardly shout. I never thought I'd see such a thing. They're all hollerin' so much they couldn't have heard me anyway. Tita squirms away from them, gets up. Finally she comes runnin' to me. Full of tears she tells me she doesn't want her pants on. The boys come over. Jazz's

nose is bleedin' into his mouth. Rock is holdin'
Tita's dirty, wet underpants. When I stop laughin'
from love I tell them they's all good children. I tell
the boys to take Tita to the creek to wash her off,
and wash out her pants, and take her home. Maybe
she has some dry underpants." Mama finished the
beer. "Whoever told those boys little girls ain't
never to be naked?"

Rafael smiled.

Mama always told stories of what had happened
that day or that night.

She had a different story every time.

Sometimes, when she was done with a story, it
was difficult for Rafael to remember where the
story had begun. Always it was difficult to understand what the story was about, or why it interested her.

*

Inside the travel trailer Rita stood near the
kitchenette wall. She was wearing the new blue and
yellow dress. It was big on her. The black plastic
belt had a new hole in it and was clinched tightly
around her waist. The tongue of the belt was many
inches long and pointed away from her. She had
put on what she called her red sandals, slippers
Rafael had found in the dump.

And she had done something to her hair, something more than just wash it. It was combed in a

special way, a way Rafael had never seen before. It looked softer, and lighter. It curved out more around her ears.

She said, "I have never had a new dress before."

He knew that.

She laughed. "I have never had two new dresses before."

Still standing, Rafael pulled off his boots. "We'll go watch the sunset."

Then Rafael noticed that Rita already had set out on the card table the big, brown plastic sheet, folded, they used for watching the sunset.

She was ready for him.

She wanted him.

His shirt and jeans removed, he fitted himself, sitting, into the bottom of the shower stall where there was still water left over from his children's and Rita's bath.

"Where's the turkey?" he asked.

"I put it in the water in the sink. I thought it would stay cooler that way."

She stood over him, looking down at his naked self, sitting, knees up, in the bottom of the shower stall. He poured water over himself with his cupped hands and used the bar of soap.

Even in the dim light, her eyes were bright and warm as she watched him bathe.

Her watching him did not have the same affect upon Rafael as had the fat old uncle staring at him

naked. Rita's eyes made him feel warm, and relaxed, a little excited, and pleasant. The uncle's
stare had made Rafael feel hot, and cold, want to
pull into himself, somehow, get behind something,
disappear, tense, and very, very tired.

"I had some of the vodka," Rita said. *She had
opened the bottle of vodka?* Rafael wondered why
that bothered him. "Is that okay?"

"Of course."

"Do you want some? I think you have not had
much to drink today. Usually, by now . . ."

"Why not?" He thought of them in a few minutes watching the sunset. "A little, maybe."

"Especially after you've been to the city. I
wasn't even expecting you back tonight, or maybe
even tomorrow."

"As long as you've opened the bottle," he said.

He stood up. With his toe, he slipped the rubber
mat away from the drain at the bottom of the
shower stall.

"There is something very different about you,"
she said.

He dried his body with the wet towel she handed
him. He felt much better after washing the sweat
and dirt and the bits of cut hair and the eyes of the
uncle off his body.

He heard the water from the shower stall pouring onto the hard-packed earth underneath the
trailer.

After he put on his new jeans, Rita held a cup with some vodka in it up to his lips. She poured it into his mouth.

He coughed.

She took the cup away and laughed. "What's the matter with you?" She drank the rest of the vodka in the cup herself.

"Everyone here drinks," Rafael said. "Even Mama. Even the children."

Rita said, "Yes."

"Everyone here is a drunk," Rafael said. "Everyone here is an alky."

"Everyone drinks as much as he has money for. Everyone drinks whatever he can get, whenever he can get it," Rita said. "There is always plenty of time for it."

"That's not the way it is everywhere," Rafael said. "I mean, not all the people in the city are as drunk."

"Some can afford drugs," Rita said. "I understand that."

Sitting on the in-built seat, Rafael pulled on his boots. "I'm an alky."

"I know."

"It has something to do with here," Rafael said. "This place."

"What else?"

Rafael put on his new shirt but did not button it. "I'm tryin' to say somethin' here, Rita."

"What?"

He had heard each of the three children coughing in their sleep in the trailer. "Will they be all right?"

"Faro will listen."

"Is she all right?"

"I gave her just a little of the vodka."

"They will be all right," Rafael said.

Rita put the big bottle of vodka in the cabinet under the sink.

*

"Listen, Rita," Rafael said. "I want everyone to get out of here. To leave this place. To leave Morgantown."

In the moonlight, the whites of her eyes were big and shining.

She stared at this idea in the night and said nothing.

They sat naked on their plastic sheet on a knoll that always had been their favorite place. It was outside the chain-link fence surrounding the dump.

As they had climbed this knoll out of sight of Morgantown, Rita and Rafael held hands. Under his free arm, Rafael carried the brown, plastic sheet.

As he walked with Rita, Rafael wondered about himself and this place and the people who were here. As a child, if there was a beer or a half a beer to be had, he drank it. If there was hard liquor to be found, almost always vodka, if someone had passed out without finishing the bottle, Rafael would sit down wherever and drink the liquor in the bottle until he, too, passed out. If there was ever more than enough for himself, he would share it with his brothers and friends. And they, too, always, drank whatever was available. He did not remember ever first doing so; he did not remember ever not doing so. It was his life, as much as were his constantly stinging eyes, constant headaches, skin rashes, running nose, coughing, his sore knuckles, his bottomless tomorrows. The miseries of hangover were twin to the miseries of not having anything to drink. He supposed his eyes stung, head ached, skin itched, nose ran, he coughed, his knuckles hurt, the future was a blank when he was drunk, but when he was drinking or drunk he felt all that less. He did not remember it. No, most of the people he saw in the city and even in Big Dry Lake did not have runny eyes and noses, rashes, did not sneeze and cough every minute, and most of them were not drunk. Most of them had jobs. And they did not live here, here, here in this place they called Morgantown.

And most of them knew, or thought they knew, were fairly sure of their futures.

For the first time, now Rafael understood that.

Now Rafael felt in control of his own life and even of his death and there was great relief in that.

At first when they had come to this knoll the dump was just being established. Over the years it had grown to take up most of its set square miles. The various mounds in the dump, for metal, for flattened cars, for tires, for glass, for this and that, had grown wider and higher. These mounds and their valleys made their own landscape of unearthly things.

As the sun set on the other side of the furtherest chain link fence, the strong, lateral rays played with and bounced off all the millions and millions of shiny things in the dump, the bits of metal and glass. The rays from the setting sun reflected as different colors, red and green, yellow, silver, even blue. As the sun lowered through the horizon, these reflections, these colors, these trillion points of light, changed, became brighter, some even stabbed their eyes, then dimmer, appeared to move from here to there. Stitching the landscape together were the yellow dirt roads the tanker and dump trucks used winding around these mounds. And here and there in the landscape were pools, some of them large, of fluids containing oils and chemicals. The low sunlight streaking these pools brought wonderful, jellied reflections of light and color from them.

After the sun fully set and the after-glow high in the eastern sky had dimmed and extinguished, Rafael and Rita undressed each other and made love slowly on their plastic sheet. They had done so over the years in this place so many times Rafael had known exactly where to place the sheet on the ground he had gradually cleared of rocks and bits of metal and glass. He supposed each of their three children had been conceived on this knoll.

After making love, they sat up. They watched the moon rise over the hill. The air they breathed had a clear, pungent, metallic odor and taste to it, seemingly sharper after their exertions. They cooled their naked bodies in the soft breeze of this heavy air.

Around the hill, ascending, ran the highway. As the moon sat on the shoulder of that hill, the headlights of the vehicles going up and down that highway seemed to pass through the moon and take their light from it.

"I want everyone to leave here," Rafael said again.

In the moonlight, Rafael read the expression on Rita's face: *How can that be?*

"My father, even your grandmother, Mama, especially the kids. You hear me?"

Rita said: "You want everyone to leave here."

"Yes," Rafael said. "Remember that."

"You're silly tonight." She sat against his

crossed ankles and rested her back against his stomach. Her shoulders were against his chest. "What are we going to do with that turkey?"

Rafael folded his arms around her ribs, just under her tiny breasts. "Cook it."

"How do you cook a turkey? There is no stove in the world big enough to cook that turkey, I think. Not even in the double wide."

Rafael thought a moment. "I guess you take it apart."

"And then what?"

Rafael thought again. "Then fry it, I guess."

"We have no propane gas, anyway. Haven't had, for almost ever."

Having propane gas Rafael associated with the luxury of having powdered coffee in hot water. Rita and he never really had had warm meals as a regular thing.

Rafael said, "Break it up and give the pieces to people who have propane gas. They will fry it and give us back some."

"Okay."

"Only don't give any to Alessandro."

"Why not?"

"I don't know. I bought him beer and suddenly he didn't like me. Maybe he resents that I bought him beer. Maybe he resents that I have a job now. Anyway, he said he didn't want any of our turkey."

"I like my dresses."

Leaning his head down to her, his face lightly brushed her hair, her cheek. "Yes?"

"They're wonderful. So pretty."

He kissed her cheekbone. "It feels good to do something for you."

"Your other presents," she said.

"What about them?"

She giggled. "They're silly."

"Why?"

"A baseball glove for an infant."

"He'll grow to fit it."

"No one here plays baseball anyway."

"People do play baseball," Rafael said. "Other places."

"Oh, yes." Rita remembered. "'Other places.'"

His right hand gave her left breast a little squeeze. "Don't you think Frankie could be a great baseball player? Why not?"

"They say next year the school bus won't even stop here. They say stopping the bus even at the entrance to the dump is too dangerous for the children already on the bus. No one goes anyway." The tips of Rafael's fingers felt in the dark for the tears he knew were on Rita's cheeks. "The children here haven't the clothes to go to school. Every morning the bus stops and waits and goes on. From now on, it won't even stop."

"It doesn't matter," Rafael said.

"To read. . ."

"They won't go to school here," Rafael said. "They'll go to school somewhere else. Somewhere they play baseball."

Rita sniffed. "A doctor set for Lina." She giggled.

"What's funny about that?"

"She's never seen a doctor. She doesn't know what a doctor does."

"The Play Doctor box will show her what a doctor does."

"We might be able to use the thermometer," Rita said.

"What do the children here play at?" Rafael asked.

"They build roads, in the dirt."

"Yeah."

"Lina babies little sticks," Rita said. "Scavenging."

"They work at that," Rafael said. "That's work."

"They pretend they're drunk and yell and fight."

The moon was higher now. It dimmed the stars and the headlights of the vehicles going up and down the highway.

Rita giggled again. "That music thing you bought Marta."

"What's wrong with that?"

"Who would teach her to play it?"

"She can teach herself. She sings little songs."

"It needs electricity."

"So?"

"We don't have electricity, silly."

"Other places have electricity."

"You're crazy." Rita turned her body to rest on her hip. She snuggled her face against Rafael's chest. "Nice crazy."

"Are the presents really wrong?" Rafael asked.

"No. They're wonderful. I have put them away in their boxes. For some day."

'Some day.' Rafael could not remember Rita ever before referring to *some day.*

"Some day," Rita now said, "now that you have a job, do you think we could go to the drag races? We have never been to the drag races. The cars speed up very fast there, burn rubber off their tires just starting to go, and the air fills with the smell and smoke of the rubber tires burning and this special fuel they use, with alcohol in it, I think. Is that right? Some of the cars go so fast parachutes are needed to stop them. If it begins to rain, all the racing cars line up on the drag strip to keep it dry. Luis has been, in his truck. And he brought Nito. Do you think you could borrow Luis' truck and take us to the drag races? We could bring the children. I'm sure they would not charge for babies."

The moonlight was diffused in Rafael's eyes. He blinked and saw the moon rounded again. *Some day.* Then the moon light diffused with the wetness in his eyes again.

"Rafael?" Rita tried to lift her head enough away from his chest to look in his face.

Rafael coughed.

"Some day," Rafael said. "Maybe with Luis."

"That would be nice."

For a long while they listened to each other's breathing.

Finally Rita moved her legs. "We must go," she said. "Before there are more flies. Before the rats find us."

"Yes." Rafael, too, began to move. "Why didn't we bring something to drink? We always do."

"You didn't seem to want it."

As Rita stood up, she said, "Make sure you give me your new shirt to wash. I want you to look nice, for Thursday."

1

"ARE YOU awake?"

Rafael answered his father: "No."

Before he opened his eyes, he smiled. That was how his father always had awakened him. And that was how Rafael always had answered him.

His father was smiling, too.

"Nito and Heyman have cut a new gap in the fence," his father said.

In the patched rope hammock stretched from a hook on the wall of his travel trailer to a crotch of a dead, dusty tree, shirtless, Rafael had been asleep. Naked, Frankie, Rafael's infant son, had been asleep curled against Rafael's side, his face, thumb in mouth, against Rafael's stomach.

The mid-morning sun had just come to fall on them. They were both sweating. It looked, and felt, and smelled, too, that Frankie had urinated a little on the skin of his father's side.

"Come with me through the fence," his father said, "I have something to show you."

Rafael yawned.

"You must take the baby out of the sun anyway," his father said.

Cradling the baby in his arms, Rafael sat up and swung his legs over the edge of the hammock.

His eyes barely open, Frankie rubbed his lips and soft nose with his little fist.

Then he began to cry.

Rafael's father smiled. "He's hungry."

Rafael said, "Of course."

Together they walked around to the front of the trailer.

Rita was just coming down the steps. "You shouldn't have had the baby in the sun, Rafael."

"I was asleep."

"He's not burnt," said his father. "Only a few minutes."

Rita took the baby into the trailer.

Rafael's father asked, "Before we go, you want to drink?"

"No. Do you?"

His father's fingers dug into a place just below his own belt. "I guess not."

As they crossed the stream to get to the chain-link fence surrounding the dump, Rafael looked to his right.

Where the stream curved and was deeper, he saw the two boys, Rock and Jazz, standing in the water. They were bathing the little girl, Tita. The day before they had been told by Mama to do that. Yesterday, there had been reason for bathing the little girl. Today they were bathing her again. Tita was naked and not protesting. The boys, silent, seemed to be being careful with her.

For a moment, Rafael wondered if he ought to stop, say something. His father did not notice the children. Rafael did not know what to say. He said nothing.

A "T" had been cut in the fence. Short wires had been twisted at the top and the middle of the cut to keep the gap closed, and to make it appear as if the fence had not been cut.

Rafael undid only the middle wire to allow him and his father to step through the gap in the fence. After they were through, he wired the gap closed again.

As father and son walked into the dump, Rafael asked his father, "What are we?"

"Uh?"

Rafael asked, "Are we Indian?"

"Has someone asked you that? Has someone asked if we are Indian?"

"Sometimes people call me an Indian," Rafael said. "Are we Hispanic?"

"No one owns us," his father said.

Rafael thought he heard a touch of anger in his father's response.

Rafael persisted. "I mean, are we white? Have we black in us? Why do people call me 'Indian?' I know nothing about all this."

"That's all," his father said. "That's enough."

Rafael stared at his shadow and at the shadow of his father as they walked along the dirt road of the dump among the hills of waste.

Finally, Rafael's father said, "Your brother, Frank, went to the army one June day. A few weeks gone from home and a mortar shell blew up nearby him. Pieces of shell entered his body. This didn't even happen in a war, but in some kind of a practice for a war that never happened. Maybe someone's careless mistake, who knows? Maybe someone did not have enough regard for your brother, Frank, as a human person to keep him out of harm's way. The pieces of metal were in his body places the doctors could not get them out. For six weeks, more or less, the inside of his body was on fire, hell burning between his toes and the top of his head. That's what his friend who saw him in the hospital said."

With a new understanding, Rafael said, "A long time to suffer."

"A long time," his father agreed. "We never knew. We would not have known, ever, if Frank's friend had not searched us out, and told us. When Luis went to the authorities to ask if this terrible news was the truth, it was still three weeks before they sent someone in uniform to us. He said they had not been able to find any such place as 'Morgantown.' He said the medal and the insurance money had been passed on to some girl Frank had

met and married on a weekend pass. We never
heard from her, either. They had been married
only a few weeks. I would not have wanted the
medal anyway, I think, but your mother might
have liked having it. Maybe your son, Frankie, one
day might have liked having it. Seems the authorities didn't have much regard for us, either."

Rafael walked along the road with his father
watching their short, mid-day shadows on the dirt.
He believed his father was taking him someplace to
show him something.

"You tell me who and what we are," his father
said. "No one owns us."

After a while, Rafael spotted a big stove on top
of a mound of metal rubble. He laughed and
pointed it out to his father. "Maybe that stove is
big enough to cook the turkey. Will we bring it
home to Rita?"

His father spat. "That turkey."

"You ever tasted turkey?"

"How much that bird cost?"

"Not much."

"Sure, I've tasted turkey. Used to be wild, when
I was a boy. Used to find 'em. How could you
afford a big, store-bought turkey like that?"

"I told you. I've got a job."

"Sure," his father said. "In a warehouse."

"Sort of a warehouse. More of a loft."

His father looked at the sweat glistening on Rafael's shoulders. "Don't you bring home any diseases, boy." He spat again. "More'n we all ready got."

Rafael climbed the pile of metal rubble. He examined the stove. Two of its four burners were gone. The oven door was connected by only one hinge. The electrical wire was badly burned.

Rafael crouched near the top of the mound, balancing on bed frames. His eye was caught by someone moving between two garbage heaps nearer the center of the dump.

A man dressed in khaki walked easily in the shade of a wide-brimmed hat. He was carrying a rifle. Also, he had a pistol holstered on his waist.

He did not see Rafael.

Rafael returned to the road where his father waited. "Ninja told no lie. There's a man over there carryin' two guns."

"No."

"I just saw him."

"Must be rats, for fun."

"In this strong light?"

"Well, he's not after us," his father said. "Who cares what we take out of the dump? It's all stuff people don't want."

Rafael, too, was puzzled why anyone dressed in khaki would be prowling the dump carrying two guns.

His father said, "We needn't fear him."

His father moved into the shade of a high hill of used tires.

Rafael asked, "What do you want to show me?"

In the shade, Rafael's father looked at his son a long moment. There seemed to be more of a question in his eyes than an answer.

"Where is it?" Rafael looked around the piles of refuse.

"Right here."

His father undid his belt. He unbuttoned the top of his fly and pulled aside the flaps. He pulled up his shirt.

Near the base of his stomach, below his belt line, was a large growth.

Rafael's father put his fingers and thumb around the lump. He held the lump to show his son it was something new to his stomach, an entity separate from his body, what had always been his body.

Rafael touched the lump on his father's stomach with his index finger. "It's hard."

"Yes."

Rafael cupped his hand, fingers spread, at the base of his own flat stomach. "I thought it was the beer finally getting to you. That you had been eating better somehow."

"How?" his father asked. "My teeth. . ."

"I know."

"Now this." His father looked down at the lump at the bottom of his stomach he held in his hand. "Eat?" he asked.

"You've only mentioned the teeth."

"Sometimes you say one thing . . ." His father fastened his fly and belt and tucked in his shirt. ". . . when there is too much to say. Who wants to hear grief?"

"Why are you telling me now? Because I have a job?"

"Nothing can be done," his father said. "I know that. Your mother had such a lump. I recognize it."

"I remember."

Rafael's father looked around the dump. "So many here."

"Cancer, I think," Rafael said. "It is cancer?"

His father shrugged. "So you will not worry about my teeth. So you will not think there is anything you or anyone else should do about them. It's not worth doing anything about my teeth, you see. So when I get drunk and cry about my teeth you will know I am not crying about my teeth."

"Do others know? Luis? Nito?"

"No."

"Why me? Why are you telling me now?"

"I worry about what you've done, Rafael."

"What have I done?"

"I don't know. You've bought your wife two new dresses. Your daughter a piano. That turkey.

You're telling everybody you bought these things from a job you haven't worked at yet."

Rafael's father waited for a response, but Rafael said nothing.

His father finally said, "I need to sit for a moment."

They both sat on tires.

Still, Rafael said nothing.

After a few minutes, Heyman came along the dirt road between the hills of refuse. In each hand he carried a car bumper. Under each arm he carried a few hubcaps. Around his neck was a coil of rusted wire. The car bumpers and hubcaps, if in good shape cleaned up, sometimes could be sold in Big Dry Lake as used car parts. Everything Heyman carried could be sold as scrap metal.

"Hey, man," Heyman said.

Holding everything, he stood in the shade of the hill of tires to visit with Rafael and his father.

Heyman held up one car bumper. "Ford." He held up the other. "Chevrolet." He laughed.

"There's a man over there carrying two guns." Rafael jerked his thumb over his shoulder.

Heyman said, "Naw."

"It's true," Rafael said.

"I was just over there," Heyman said. "There's nobody."

"The manager, I think," Rafael said. "He carries guns."

"He fixed the fence," his father said.

"They always fix the fence." Heyman smiled.

"They've never carried guns before," Rafael said.

"I tell you, I was just over there," Heyman said.

"I saw him. From up there." Rafael pointed above, behind him to the top of the hill of loose metal.

Rafael's father siad, "I don't believe him, either. There are too many rats to shoot. They are not worth the bullets."

"Okay," Rafael said.

"See you." Heyman carried his junk metal in the direction of the gap in the fence.

"Okay," Rafael said. "Be careful."

There was more silence between Rafael and his father after Heyman left.

Finally, his father said to Rafael, "I am sorry if I made you sad."

And, finally, Rafael said, "We all have to die."

Looking at his son from under his lowered eyelids, his father said, "You are not that hard, Rafael. You are protecting yourself."

Rafael said, "Mama took a long time to die. She suffered a long time."

"Yes."

"That's what matters, isn't it?"

"What?"

"And what do you get for your death? For your suffering?"

"What good am I? I have never known."

"What good is your death?"

"You're crying, Rafael." His father put his hand on Rafael's hand. "That's all right."

"What am I crying for?" Abruptly, Rafael stood up.

"It's all right to cry, Rafael. That is not what I meant. I just want you to be careful. There is Rita. The children . . ."

"Yes," Rafael said.

A loud shot startled them both.

His father said, "A gun?"

There was a second shot.

A boy's voice was crying loudly something incomprehensible.

Rafael began running toward the sound of the voice.

"Rafael!" his father shouted.

Ninja was slipping and sliding down a high hill of garbage. One of his arms was flailing, his hand grabbing for the calf of his right leg. Rafael saw the boy's blood gushing down his bare leg. Ninja's other hand clutched a plastic table radio.

At the base of the hill of garbage, Ninja fell face down on the dirt road.

By the time Rafael reached him, Ninja had rolled

onto his back. He was holding his bleeding calf in the grip of one hand. His other hand still held onto the plastic radio tightly.

Ninja saw Rafael.

"Shit, it hurts!" Ninja's lips were bubbling saliva.

Rafael pulled Ninja's fingers from the wound. Through a little blood, Rafael could see the smooth, indented entry wound of the bullet on the inside of Ninja's leg. Through much more blood, he could see the bigger exit wound on the outside of his leg. The skin around the exit wound was shredded.

"Yeow!" Ninja howled.

Rafael said, "Shut up!"

His father knelt beside Rafael. He wrapped his belt around Ninja's leg above his knee.

"The bullet went clean through," Rafael said.

Now Ninja was crying. His deep, dark eyes glistened in the bright sunlight. He sucked in breath through his nose and blew bubbles through his lips making a noise Rafael had never heard before.

Divested of all the scrap metal that had been hanging from him, Heyman stood over Ninja. His hands were on his knees. He was a little out of breath.

He said, "Hey, man," to the boy writhing on the ground.

"The bullet went clean through," Rafael said.

His father was trying to make his narrow belt hold a knot above the boy's knee. "Let's get him out of here."

"Hey, look," Heyman said.

At the place that stretch of dirt road curved between two hills of rubbish, in the shade stood the man dressed in khaki. His rifle was in the crook of his arm. Beneath the wide brim of his hat, standing still, the man watched them.

Rafael jumped up. "You son of a bitch!" He yelled at the man. "You shot a boy!"

The man remained perfectly still.

Rafael grabbed a handful of dirt off the road and threw it toward the man. Some of the dirt went in Rafael's own eyes.

Still the man did not move, or speak.

"Bastard!" Rafael yelled.

"Yeow, shit, fuck," the boy said quietly.

Rafael's father was trying to help Heyman lift Ninja from the ground.

Pushing his father aside, Rafael grabbed Ninja's shoulders. His hands were in the boy's arm pits.

"Goddamn it, Ninja," Rafael said. "Drop the damned radio!"

As they walked, Rafael's father forced the radio out of the tight grip of the boy's hand. He tossed it to the side of the road.

Carrying Ninja's feet, Heyman looked back over his shoulder at the man carrying the rifle.

Then, as they went along, Rafael's father tried to keep his belt tight around the boy's leg. He pressed his thumb into the exit wound.

Still, as Rafael carried Ninja's shoulders, the boy's head propped against his stomach, Rafael saw plenty of blood splattering the ground.

By the time they had carried Ninja through the gap in the fence across the stream and into the store and laid him on the counter, all the boy's skin, especially his face, had whitened. His eyelids were fluttering.

As they had passed the window of Mama's crate, she had begun screaming out the news of Ninja's being hurt, being shot, bleeding. Everyone must have heard the two loud shots.

Rafael noticed Father Stratton's black Buick parked in the shade of the hillside below the highway.

Shortly after they laid Ninja on the counter, almost everyone in the community was in the store or standing just outside.

Rafael had to dodge his way through the people to get out of the store.

Father Stratton grabbed his arm. "Where are you going, Rafael?"

"The man shot him. He just shot him. Shot Ninja's leg."

Still holding tightly onto Rafael's arm, Father

Stratton said, "I want you to come to confession, Rafael."

The smell of alcohol came from the priest's mouth. The priest was liked and respected by everyone Rafael knew because he was a drinker, too. It was what the priest had in common with these people.

"Yes, Father."

"I mean, this afternoon." The priest's eyes seemed fierce with seriousness.

Rafael jerked his arm free. "Yes, Father. All right!"

"Rafael! Aren't you helping?"

From the sunlight outside the store, Rafael looked at the crowd of people in the store hovering around Ninja.

"No," Rafael said. "There are enough people helping. I do not need. . . I do not want. . ."

"You hate to see suffering, don't you, Rafael?"

Rafael began coughing into his hands.

Within seconds, he was on his knees not far from the priest's feet vomiting.

m

"BLESS ME, Father, for I have sinned," Rafael said into the grille of the cool, dark confessional box.

And then he stopped.

"How long since your last confession, Rafael?"

"I don't know. Do you remember? Have I stopped when I was coming home from the city drunk and confessed?"

"Yes."

"When was the last time I did that?"

Father Stratton said, "I don't remember, either."

"Well, that was the last time then," Rafael said.

"Do you remember the last time you came to confession sober?"

"God, no."

"Because there's always the question whether doing penance when you are drunk works."

"You shouldn't pray when you're drunk?"

Father Stratton sighed.

"Because I've always done penance," Rafael said.

Through the grille came the smell of stale liquor from the priest's mouth. For the first time, Rafael wondered if he was smelling the priest's rotting liver.

After leaving Ninja on the store counter in the care of other people, Rafael had gone to his travel trailer. He poured himself five or six ounces of liquor from the big vodka bottle.

He sat on the single bed he and Rita shared, his back against the wall, his knees up.

He gulped most of his drink and felt instantly ill. Tightening his jaw, his stomach muscles, he finished the drink.

The only effect it had upon him was to make his stomach churn.

His father had a lump in his stomach similar to the lump that had killed his mother. She suffered greatly, for a long time. There could never be enough money for doctors or the comfort they could bring. There never had been.

Rafael was glad he would not live to see his father suffer so, and for so long.

People sneaking into the dump now to take things out of it, to eat, to live, were liable to be shot. The authorities did not want them taking things no one else wanted from the dump. The dump manager had shot Ninja, a boy, in the leg. Rafael remembered Ninja's tight grip on the old, broken, plastic radio.

No doctor would see to Ninja, either.

Rafael put his empty cup on the floor. To some

of this, he had the solution. He needed to stay
sober, awake, work on his own future, his own
salvation, the future and salvation of many.

He wandered back outside into the sunlight.
People were still milling around the store, talking
in shock and worry and anger about what had
happened to Ninja, to all of them. Rafael did not
look into the cooler darkness of the store.

Father Stratton's black Buick was gone. Maybe
Rafael could have ridden to the church with him.

Carrying his shirt, Rafael walked up to the highway and down along its shoulder to where it flattened outside the dump entrance. He turned to face
the traffic. Walking backward, he put out his
thumb. He had discovered drivers were quicker to
pick him up, if at all, if he was not wearing a shirt.
This afternoon one of the first vehicles to pass him
stopped to give him a ride.

He had put on his shirt before entering the cool
of the church in Big Dry Lake.

"All right, Rafael," Father Stratton said through
the grille in the confession box. "Tell me your sins."

"Drunkenness," Rafael said.

"Yes," Father Stratton said. "How many
times?"

"Whenever."

"Whenever you can, is that right?"

"Yes. But I haven't felt much like a drink lately,
when I've had it to drink."

"Since when?"

"Yesterday afternoon."

"Are you telling me you've had nothing to drink since yesterday afternoon?"

"No."

"You just haven't been drunk—"

"When I could have been."

"It won't do any good to talk to you about drinking, will it?"

"No."

"You're young, Rafael. Very young. You have your whole life ahead of you." *I have tomorrow, and Thursday morning*, Rafael thought. "You have Rita and the children." *That's too true*, Rafael thought, *too true*. "Oh, well. . . Are you faithful to Rita, Rafael?"

"Yes."

"You have had sex with no one else?"

"Who?"

"Anyone. Such as, anyone in the city."

"No."

"All right, Rafael, tell me your other sins."

Rafael hesitated. "I don't always know what I do when I'm drunk. I might sin then, and not know it. I don't remember."

"You say you were not drunk yesterday afternoon?"

"Not really drunk."

"You remember clearly everything you did yesterday afternoon?"

Larry, the fat uncle, the barbershop, the bank, the woman there, the big store where he went shopping, the things he bought, the two men, the woman who helped Rafael, the cashier, wheeling his presents down the street in the shopping cart, Freedo, the big bottle of vodka, the bus ride, getting off the bus, Rita climbing up to the road to meet him, her face as she saw the two new dresses, Lina tumbling down the slope, his giving the presents to the children, buying drinks for everyone at the store, his climbing the knoll with Rita, the sun, the moon, Rafael remembered it all with more clarity than he remembered most times of his life. "Yes, Father."

"Rafael, where did you get so much money?" Rafael did not answer. "Do not lie in the confessional box, Rafael."

"I got a job, Father."

"From what I hear, you did not do a job, Rafael. You just got money. You bought dresses for your wife, presents for your children, a big turkey."

"I have the right to do that."

"If you have the money."

"I had the money."

"New clothes for yourself. Where did you get the money, Rafael?"

"I did some of the job yesterday."

"Rafael, what did you do for so much money?"

"I took my clothes off. This fat, old man. . ."

"Did he touch you?"

"Yes. He touched himself more. He did not touch me in the way you mean."

"What did he do?"

"He just talked crazy. He excited himself. He described crazy things." Rafael was surprised to hear himself saying these things. Was he lying in the confessional? How could he explain to the priest, how could he tell him more, the whole truth? He could not explain about the contract, and the bank account, and the card the woman in the bank wanted Rita to sign so she could get the money, later. "The fat old man just got excited as he talked and waved his arms around, and smelled worse."

"You said you did *part* of the job yesterday."

"Yes."

"Does this man expect you to come back?"

"Yes."

"Do not go back to him, Rafael."

Rafael thought. "I cannot steal, Father."

"We are not talking about stealing. You cannot get money this way, Rafael, and you cannot steal it, either. Do not go back to this man, Rafael."

"You saw that the man in the dump shot Ninja."

"Yes. I saw that."

"The children are sick and hungry. We are all sick. My father will die from a lump in his stomach, the way my mother did."

"Rafael, do not go back to this man."

"I am not committing the crime, Father."

"What crime?"

"Any crime."

"You have always been a good boy, Rafael. When Rita became with child, you married her as soon as I said to. Isn't that true?"

"Yes, Father."

"There are many temptations, my son. Drinking yourself drunk. Stealing from the dump."

"'Stealing?'"

"Be glad there is confession, and forgiveness. I cannot absolve you of your sins, Rafael, unless you truly intend, in your heart, to commit these sins no more."

"Father? I really believe I will not be drunk again. Or take things from the dump."

"You're a good boy, Rafael. Do you remember your prayers, that Sister taught you?"

"Pretty well."

"This is your penance." The priest told Rafael to say certain prayers, by name, how many times each prayer, before he left the church. "And Rafael? Do not go back to that man."

Without saying anything more, Rafael left the confession box.

He knelt in a pew at the front of the church, near the altar. The Stations of the Cross, raised and painted plaster depictions of the suffering of Jesus Christ at the time of His crucifixion, were placed on the side walls of the church, seven to a side.

Over the altar at the front of the church was a crucifix. The painted plaster Jesus hanging on the cross was life sized.

The figure was naked, except for a loin cloth.

Blood oozed from His feet, one atop the other, held to the cross by a single nail. Blood poured from His side, where He had been stabbed by a sword. Blood dripped from the palms of His hands, where they had been nailed to the cross beam. Blood dribbled from where the thorns of the crown placed upon His head had cut into His scalp.

As Rafael repeated his prayers in penance again and again, kneeling in a front pew, he found himself staring at the crucifixion. He had been familiar with this particular depiction of Christ's suffering all his life.

"*'I thirst. Give Me to drink. . .' And He was given a sponge soaked in wine. . . Three hours He suffered. . .*"

Rafael's rote repetition of his prayers of penance slowed and then stopped as he stared at the crucifixion.

Jesus Christ. . . I'm gonna end up a bloodier mess than You.

n

"THEY CAME and took the big bottle of vodka," Rita said.

She stood in the kitchenette area of the trailer.

"Who?"

"Your brother. Nito." Rita looked down at the cracked linoleum on the floor. "He said your father sent him for it. Old Callie wanted to use some of it to clean Ninja's wound, he said."

"When?"

"Hours ago."

"No one brought it back?"

"No."

"That's okay."

Rita's eyes lightened as she looked into Rafael's face.

Rafael had walked the miles from Big Dry Lake. He had not tried to get a ride. In the late afternoon heat, walking along the dirt shoulder of the highway felt good to him. He felt more alive than he remembered ever feeling.

Rita asked, "Will you get the buckets of water for me?"

"Yes," Rafael answered. "I'm very thirsty."

As Rafael entered the store after fetching the buckets of water for his children's and Rita's baths, Alessandro was saying something about 'reward.'

Again the conversation stopped when Rafael entered.

The big bottle of vodka was on the concrete floor in the middle of the group sitting there in the late afternoon. The bottle was nearly empty.

Rafael's father looked up at Rafael with wary, bloodshot eyes.

"Mind if I have some?" Rafael picked up the bottle. He poured some vodka into a paper cup.

"It's your vodka," Marie said slowly.

Rafael placed the bottle back on the floor, where it had been.

"Tell us about Ninja," Alessandro said. "The man in the dump."

Rafael leaned against a pile of empty boxes. "Yesterday, Ninja told no lie. There is a man in the dump carrying two guns, a rifle and one on his hip. He is dressed in khaki clothes and wears a wide-brimmed hat."

"Ah," his father said. "Everyone is a cowboy. Except us."

"You saw him?" Marie asked.

"Yes. From the top of a heap. I don't think he saw me. I tried to tell Heyman about him but he

didn't believe me. I never saw Ninja. I didn't know
he was in the dump."

"Was the man wearing any kind of a badge?"
Rider asked.

"I didn't see no badge," Rafael answered.

"You don't need no badge to shoot at us, I
reckon," his father said.

Rafael said, "No, I didn't see no badge even
when the bastard stood close to us, after he shot
Ninja, while he was watching us carry Ninja off. I
swore at him."

"Yes, you did." His father slid his fingers under
his belt. "You swore at him good."

"The new dump manager," Alessandro said.

"I ran to where I heard Ninja screaming. He was
sort of falling down a garbage hill." Rafael looked
into his paper cup. "Did the vodka help clean the
wound?"

"He'll be hoppin'," Old Callie said. "Rest of his
natural days."

Marie said, quietly, "If he doesn't lose the leg
entire-like."

"I did a good job, cleanin' and bindin' that
wound, both sides and in between," Callie said.
"Good as I could do, anyway."

Callie had no training at nursing anyone had
ever heard of but she had a willingness to nurse the
sick and wounded which caused people to hope she
was some good at it.

"While you and Heyman and your father were carrying Ninja off, this man with the guns stood close to you and watched?" Alessandro asked.

"Yes."

"But he didn't raise his guns to you then?"

"No."

"Rafael swore at him good," Rafael's father said.

"He didn't make like he was going to shoot at the rest of you then?"

"He just watched us."

"We can get that guy easy enough." Rider hitched up his jeans with his one good hand.

Rider had flown off the highway one night on his motorcycle. He landed face down in the dust just above Morgantown. Jazz had found him in the morning. Both Rider and his motorcycle were badly broken. The motorcycle never moved again. Rider recovered enough to limp around, bones in his face, legs, some ribs broken. His left arm was now useless to him. Sometimes, laughing, he would tell the story of taking flight off the edge of the highway in the dark. He always said it was the greatest thing he had ever done, the greatest, most free feeling he had ever had. He said he wished he could afford another motorcycle, so he could try it again.

"Tell me, Rafael," Alessandro said, "Had Ninja found anything, was he taking anything particularly wonderful from the dump? Gold? Jewelry? Cash money?"

Rafael shrugged. Such a question was not worth answering.

In Rafael's opinion, Alessandro frequently spoke foolishly, asked foolish questions. Everyone knew Alessandro could read and write. When he first arrived he said he had been, at one time in his life, a school coach and a school teacher. After being there a while, Alessandro had been the one to go to town and again try to get the power company to turn the electricity on to the store. He told the power company he personally would collect the money from the people to pay the bill when it came. There was not enough cash money to give the power company up front to make them believe Alessandro. Soon he stopped telling people he had been, at one time in his life, a school coach and school teacher. Sometimes he still said foolish things and asked foolish questions.

Rafael's father answered. "A little brown radio. He held it so tight I had to whip it out of his hand." Loosely, he flapped his arm to show how he had shaken Ninja's arm to loosen his grip on the plastic radio.

"We know the dump better'n he does," Rider said. "We can get him, easy."

"Big talk," Nito said.

Old Callie, clutching her lose dress to her stomach with one hand, bent over and poured more vodka into her cup, which she had placed on the floor.

"We can," Rider said.

"Sure."

As Callie stood erect, she drank from her cup. She swayed, dizzily.

Marie said, "Dance for us, Callie."

Gray hair brushing her cheeks, Callie did a little dance step on the uneven floor.

"That's what Father Stratton came to say to us this afternoon," Mrs. Woburn said.

Alessandro sighed.

Old Callie flopped into her chair as exhausted as if she had danced away the night.

"What?" Rider said.

Mrs. Woburn shifted her purse in her lap. "That we are to stay out of the dump."

Mrs. Woburn had never let on anything about herself. Rafael could not remember exactly when or how she had arrived in Morgantown. She had never said more about herself than, "I am Mrs. Woburn." No first name, no information about whether she was a widow, divorced, mother, daughter, sister, friend, had held a job, been in any institution, punitive, curative; simply: "I am Mrs. Woburn" was all she had ever said about herself, her world, her place in it.

And she always carried a purse, a small one, with brass bars running along its top which clasped together. Never had she been seen to open the purse, look in it, put anything in it, take anything out of it.

Nor had Mrs. Woburn ever been seen, or known, to take a drink of any kind of liquor.

"He has always come to say that," Alessandro said.

"This time he means it. He says the town fathers mean it."

Rafael's father asked his son, "Did you go to the church in Big Dry Lake this afternoon to see Father Stratton?"

"Yes."

"Did you confess your sins?"

"Yes."

"Do you feel better now?"

"I feel better, now."

"Ah, the young," Rafael's father said. "They can do anything."

Mrs. Woburn said, "Father Stratton says they are serious now."

"They are always serious," Alessandro said.

"They have fixed the fence again," Mrs. Woburn said. "And the manager of the dump has been given guns and orders to shoot."

Rafael's father said, "They had already shot Ninja."

Her head against the back of her chair, Old Callie began to sing *Blue Moon*.

Tears were starting in Rafael's father's eyes. "What else are we to do?"

"Go," Rafael said.

Alessandro was the first to look hard at Rafael, then Rider, Mrs. Woburn, Nito, and finally, his father.

Old Callie continued singing. She was appreciated in Morgantown for her sweet, thin voice.

Rafael shifted his back against the boxes. "Get out of here."

Alessandro said, "A bus is picking us all up in the morning, to take us to the airport. We are being flown to the capitol, where we will all be fed. Then a special plane will take us to Paris, France."

Rider said, "Wish I had a bike." He laughed.

"There are the children," Rafael's father said. "Rock, Tita, Jazz, Sammy . . ."

"We cannot even go to Big Dry Lake," Alessandro said.

Rafael's father said, "The young . . ."

"I'm serious," Rafael said.

Marie said, "We're all serious, Rafael. If we cannot pick the dump. . ."

"Why can't we?" Rafael's father asked. "That land belonged to Morgan. . ."

"They don't want us to get hurt there," Alessandro said. "So they shoot us."

"I'm gonna whack that guy," Rider said.

"It's time to go." Rafael put his paper cup, which he had emptied, on a carton next to him.

Then he remained standing there. The eyes of most of the people again swiveled slowly to him.

Rafael said, "It's time to go."

He left the store.

*

"Earlier today, I spoke to your brother. Luis," Rita said, "about carrying us sometime to the drag races, when he goes, now that you have a job, and all, money to pay our way in."

Rafael said nothing.

When Rafael had returned to the travel trailer Rita told him to change his jeans. "You've got Ninja's blood all over them. Tomorrow I'll wash them and your new shirt so you'll look clean and nice Thursday when you go to the city to do your job." While Rafael changed his jeans, Rita made them baloney sandwiches and stirred some powdered tea into glasses of creek water for them to drink.

They sat together on the steps of their trailer munching and drinking.

Rafael had not put on his boots.

"Tomorrow," Rita said, "I'll try to get that big turkey fried."

"Good."

"Rafael," Rita said, "how can the people here live, if we can't pick the dump?"

"We can't."

"If they mean to shoot us. . ."

"That's what they're talkin' about at the store."

"Everybody's talkin' about it."

"That's what Father Stratton came out to tell us this afternoon. The dump manager has orders to shoot us."

"He was a little late."

"You know him."

"I wonder why he drinks. He has a Buick car and lives in a house, has clean clothes and extra flesh."

"You know priests can't make love."

"Why is that?"

"To make them different, I guess."

"That's crazy. It is the only good thing."

"They don't have to worry about women and children. It is easy for them."

"That's my only thought," Rita said.

"What is?"

"That only women and children pick the dump from now on."

"What?"

"That the men stay out of the dump."

"What sense does that make?"

"Surely they wouldn't shoot women and children."

"They shot Ninja. He's just a kid. What is he, fourteen?"

"Twelve, but he's tall."

"How could you carry things?"

"We could drag them to the fence. Mrs. Woburn's strong. So is Marie, sometimes. I'm strong enough."

"Rita, you remember what I said last night?"

"What?"

"The people have got to get out of here."

"How? Only Luis' truck works. Mama would about fill up the back of the truck all by herself."

"Take buses. Hitch rides. Walk. Get out of here."

"Go where?"

"Anywhere."

"To the city? Beg? Let the little children beg and learn to steal? Sleep on the sidewalks at night like all those other people? We've seen them. How is that better? The little children here now don't beg and steal."

"They won't have to beg and steal. Get everyone cleaned up. New clothes. Maybe split up. Everyone go somewhere different where maybe the authorities would help people along and get jobs."

"Where's that at?" Rita asked.

Rafael thought, *What in fact to do with Mama, Rita's grandmother?* Physically the old, fat woman really couldn't move. *What about some of the children, who really belonged to no one?*

"Rita? My father has a lump like the one that killed my mother. In his stomach."

"So has Francine. She never leaves the double wide anymore."

"Did you know about my father?"

Luis' truck was bouncing down the road from the highway. In the raised dust behind the truck was another car.

"Everyone here is sick," Rita said. "The children. . ."

Luis was being followed by a police car.

"Ol' Luis must have been speedin'," Rafael said.

"They can't take his license away from him. He hasn't got one."

The people in Morgantown had little regard or fear of the police. The courts knew the people here could not pay fines, surrender driver's licenses they didn't have, and that time served in the jailhouse only meant showers, clean clothes and some food every day. Except for obstreperous, drunken behavior within the city limits of Big Dry Lake they could not ignore, the police left the citizens of Morgantown pretty well alone.

Rita said, "Your father. . ." Frowning, she stared into the dirt at the bottom of the trailer steps and said no more.

Rafael said, "I know. I guess I know."

Luis got out of his pick-up truck. Hands on hips, he waited for the police car to stop.

Two police officers got out of the car. They slipped their night-sticks through their belt loops. One released the strap holding his pistol in its holster.

Luis pointed across to where Rita and Rafael were sitting on their trailer's steps.

Both officers looked across at Rafael.

They ambled toward Rafael and stopped in front of him.

"You have a big bottle of vodka, Rafael?" one of them asked.

"I did have."

"Where is it?"

Rafael pointed. "In the store."

One went to fetch the big vodka bottle.

"Where'd you ever get a big bottle of vodka, Rafael?"

"Someone gave it to me."

"Who?"

"A bartender in the city."

"He *gave* it to you?"

"Yes."

"What was it, your birthday or something?"

"No."

"Sure."

With the big vodka bottle dangling from a crooked finger, the other officer returned. He was shaking his head. "Goddamned dump pickers," he said. "They're all drunk in there. Two are passed out in chairs, and one's on the floor."

"They're not all drunk," Rafael said. "Mrs. Woburn. . ."

"You drunk right now, Rafael?" the first officer

asked. He picked up Rafael's tea and sniffed it. "Stinks."

The second officer held up the empty vodka bottle. "This yours?"

"It was," Rafael said. "You can have it."

"You know the Real Liquor Store, Rafael?"

"Which one is that?"

"The big one. This side of Big Dry Lake."

"Sure."

"You been in there?"

"Sure"

"Were you in there yesterday afternoon?"

"No."

"Where were you yesterday afternoon, Rafael?"

"City."

"Sure."

"How did you get back?"

"Bus."

"What time?"

"The three-thirty bus."

"You've been spending money, haven't you? Presents for everybody."

Rafael's brother, Luis, stood behind the police officers. His arms were folded across his chest.

"Where'd you get so much cash money, Rafael?"

Rafael did not say anything.

"That woman in the liquor store you shot,

Rafael, died eight hours later. Did you know that?"

Beside Rafael, Rita's face had drained of color. Her mouth hung open.

Rafael said, "That's a long time to suffer."

"I'll say it is," the second police officer said.

"What did you do with the gun, Rafael?"

Rafael said, "I saw the police around and inside the liquor store through the window while I was ridin' on the bus."

The second officer held the vodka bottle up. "You got this bottle from the liquor store, didn't you Rafael? You robbed the store of money and then shot the woman because you wanted the bottle of liquor. You couldn't resist, could you?"

"No."

"You shot a woman, murdered her, for a drink."

Rafael kept looking at his brother.

"Come on."

The second officer grabbed Rafael by the shoulder and helped him stand up and away from the trailer steps.

The first officer cuffed Rafael's wrists behind his back.

Rafael said to Luis: "Why you doing me this way, bro'?"

Luis said, "You did it, Rafael. Don't ask me nothin'."

Rita fell forward off the step, onto the dirt.

"Jeez," the second officer said. "Another one passed out. No wonder there are never any lights down here at night. They're all passed out."

"Can't I pick her up?" Rafael asked.

The second officer, with the empty vodka bottle dangling from one hand, held onto Rafael's arm. "We're gettin' outta here. This place really stinks."

Rafael was walked to the police car and put into the back seat. Mama saw them as they passed. She said nothing. Rock and Tita watched. Mrs. Woburn watched from the door of the store.

From the back seat of the police car, Rafael looked at Rita face down in the dirt where the children always played.

He heard the first police officer saying to Luis, "You get the money after your brother's convicted. Don't bother us about it until then. You hear me, shitface? Don't bother us."

O

"Now, WHAT have we here?" The man who eventually came to the room where Rafael had been brought in the morning was short. A soft stomach held his white shirt out over his belt. His face was jowly. Bald on top of his head, light white hair curled out over his ears. Behind his glasses, his blue eyes twinkled with apparent humor and friendliness. He reminded Rafael of drawings he had seen in books for children. "Robbery with a deadly weapon. First degree murder. My, my. You appear to be in a peck of trouble, Rafael."

At the table, cater-cornered to the man, Rafael sat forward on a hard, plastic chair. He had been waiting a long time in that room.

"I'm not," Rafael said. "I did nothin'."

The man's happy eyes fixed on Rafael's face. "Don't you think you'd better have a lawyer with you, son? I'm about to ask you some questions."

"Ask 'em."

"You won't have to pay for the lawyer yourself."

Hands on his biceps, Rafael tried not to shiver. "I don't know nothin' about lawyers."

179

"As the Scotch minister said, 'Nevertheless. . .'
You waive your rights?"

"I was on the three-thirty bus from the city. I
saw the cops swarmin' the liquor store as I went
by."

Sliding a few papers from his folder around on
the table, the man said, "It's been reported you said
that. And you were carrying packages on the bus?"

"Yes. And the bottle of vodka."

"Exactly what was in the packages you were
carrying, Rafael?"

Rafael envisioned all the wonderful things that
had been in the shopping cart he had trundled
down the street. "They weren't wrapped."

"No?"

"Two dresses for Rita. Presents for my kids."

"Rita is your wife?"

"Yes."

"Your legal wife? I mean, have you ever really
married her?"

"Yes."

"How many kids do you have, Rafael?"

"Three."

"How can you support three kids?"

Rafael shifted in his chair. "Pickin' the dump.
Yesterday the man in the dump shot Ninja."

"What's a Ninja?"

"A kid. A twelve year old kid. How is that fair?"

"'Fraid I don't know what you're talking about."

"Isn't it a crime to shoot somebody?"

"Usually," the man said.

"Why aren't you talkin' to the man who shot Ninja?"

"How many kids do you plan to have, Rafael?" Receiving no answer, the man said, "You don't plan, do you? You just go bouncing along, like a mongrel cur dog. Have you always lived in Morgantown?"

"Yes," Rafael said. "No. I don't know."

The man was writing on one of the pieces of paper. "You use drugs, Rafael?"

"I drink."

"No other drugs?"

"I smoke."

"Marijuana?"

"There's never been much around."

"You can blame us for that. Do you use hard stuff? Peyote, mescaline? Chemicals?"

"Where would I find any of that?"

Looking at his papers, the man said, "You sure have been in jail a lot for bein' drunk. I don't see that there have ever been any other charges against you: car theft, burglary, mugging. . ."

"I don't do none of that stuff."

"If you had done any of those things drunk, we would have caught you for sure."

"I've never done nothin' like all that."

Rafael gave in to a shiver spasm.

"Would you like a drink now?"

"Yes."

"You'd like to drink any time, wouldn't you. . . Any time you can get it, I expect." Rafael shrugged. "Besides dump pickin', you ever had a job, a real job?"

"Workin' on my brother's truck."

The man consulted another piece of paper. "Would that be your brother Luis?"

"Yes."

"Can you read and write, Rafael?"

"Not so good."

"Let's get back to the packages you say you were carrying on the bus. What else were you carrying?"

"Presents for my kids."

"What were they?"

"A music thing for Marta."

"Some kind of a musical instrument?"

"Yeah. A piano thing. A Play Doctor box for Lina. A baseball glove for Frankie. My brother was killed in the army."

"How old are these children?"

"Little."

"How old is this Frankie you brought this baseball glove for?"

"Little. A baby. Born this year."

Eyes twinkling, the man gave Rafael a full smile. "You're providing for their future."

Rafael felt his face grow hot.

The man noticed. His eyebrows rose.

Rafael shivered.

"Sorry, Rafael," he said. "If I had a drink right now, I still couldn't give it to you. Are you all right?"

"Let's get done," Rafael said. "Rita is goin' to fry the turkey today."

"Fry a turkey?"

"Yeah. Isn't that how you cook 'em?"

The man said, "I guess you can fry anything. Did you have this turkey on the bus with you?"

"Yeah."

"And a big bottle of vodka, supposedly."

"Yeah."

"A gallon bottle?"

"A big bottle," Rafael said. "The biggest."

"Where did you get these presents, Rafael?"

"At that big, big store in the city with the big, big parking lot."

"What's the name of that store?"

"I forget."

"You don't know the name of the store because you've never been able to read it. Isn't that right?" When Rafael did not answer, the man asked, "And why weren't these presents wrapped?"

"The cashier woman didn't put them in bags."

"Why not?"

"Some men came along. They thought I was stealin' those things."

"And were you?"

"No. I had the money to pay for them."

Looking at his papers, the man said, "Your brother Luis says you even bought yourself some new clothes."

"Jeans. A shirt."

The man pointedly looked at the jeans Rafael was wearing. They had been worn thin. The only substance to them was the irremovable grease.

Rafael had been brought to the county police station in Big Dry Lake without a shirt and without his boots.

He had been fingerprinted and photographed and put in a cell by himself.

All night he had sat on his bunk with his back in the corner of the cell, his arms wrapped around himself, shivering violently from the air-conditioning.

It had been a long night. It was the first night, ever, he had been away from home not drunk or passed out somewhere. He envisioned the Morgantown store, the inside and the outside of it; Mama looking through the little window from her bed inside the crate; the travel trailer where he lived; Lina and Marta playing around the trailer. . . Rita fainted and fallen face down in the dust where the children played.

In the morning, a young man dressed in khaki brought Rafael two bowls. In one was warm porridge. In the other, hot, strong coffee. Rafael appreciated that.

After eating, he shivered even more.

Most of the morning was gone when an old man, dressed in a blue police uniform, brought him to this room with the table and two chairs. Leaving Rafael alone in the room, the man closed and locked the door. Feeling the cold from the air-conditioning ducts, Rafael waited another hour or two in the room.

"Why did the men in the store think you were stealing things?"

"I don't know. I was wearing the new clothes. The tags were still on them. I told the cashier about them, but she pushed a button anyway."

The man looked thoughtfully at Rafael. "I wouldn't want you in my store, either. If I had a store."

Rafael fixed the man in the eye.

"You say you had the money for these things. You paid for them. These men let you go. But your presents were not wrapped."

"Yes."

"Where did you get the money, Rafael? Sounds to me like you spent hundreds of dollars." At Rafael's silence, the man asked, "Dump pickin'? Does dump pickin' pay that well? Did you find something especially valuable in the dump?"

"I got a job."

"Really!"

"Yeah."

"That brings us to your mythical job."

"Magical job? It's not a magical job."

"Did you get the job of president of the insurance company? I didn't hear you were elected mayor. . ."

"I have a job to do," Rafael said. "It's in a loft."

The man poised his pen over a sheet of paper. "Employer's name?"

Rafael hesitated. "Mister McCarthy."

"Name of company? Address? Telephone number?" Each time Rafael did not answer, the man waited patiently. "You have a job, but you don't know where. Doing what? What is your job, Rafael? Moving crates? Moving drugs? Selling them?" He looked at Rafael's face, his shoulders, chest, stomach. "Something sexual? I can't think of anything sexual you could do to get that much money that fast." The man dropped his pen on the table. "Come on, Rafael. You're accused of robbing a liquor store. Of murdering a young woman. Your own brother came to the police station yesterday afternoon and turned you in. I'm tryin' to help you, boy. I'm your friend. You've got to help me out here. Tell me where you got the money and I'll try to prove it and maybe find out you're innocent and let you go home to your fried turkey."

Rafael said, "Mister McCarthy gave me some money."

"You know this man? Ever seen him before? Is he some kind of relative?"

"No."

The man sighed. "Okay, Rafael. Tell me about the gallon jug of vodka."

"Someone gave it to me."

"Who?"

There was a knock on the door.

Rafael said, "Freedo."

The young man who had brought Rafael the porridge and the coffee that morning opened the door enough to put his head inside the room. "Someone here to see you."

"Who?" the man asked.

"The priest. Father Stratton."

"Tell him I confessed Saturday, took Communion Sunday, and even put five dollars in the plate."

"He says it concerns - " The young man nodded his head at Rafael.

The man looked Rafael fully in the face. "Rafael, when I come back, tell me something. Anything. Make up a story. Give me something to investigate. Okay?"

He went into the corridor.

As the man stepped through the door, Rafael

heard Father Stratton's voice. "John, you're wasting your time. . ."

The policeman held the door open a crack, leaned on it, probably so it would not latch, lock itself.

Rafael heard snatches of the conversation in the corridor. Father Stratton said, "This is a good boy. . . He's too stupid to hold up a liquor store. . . He couldn't organize it. . . Where could he get a working gun?" The policeman said something about the big bottle of vodka. Father Stratton said, "I know he had money, bought presents. . . I'm pretty sure I know where and how he got the money. You understand me, John? I can say no more. Not from that liquor store murder. . ."

Suddenly there was a different, louder voice: "It's my day off!"

The police man said, "We appreciate your comin' in."

"I had a choice?" the loud voice asked. "Police car in my driveway! I was takin' my kid to the lake. Suddenly this police car! My wife thinks I'm in trouble with the police!"

"Just want you to identify someone. . ." The policeman swung the door open.

"Bringin' me all the way out here on my day off. . . !"

From where he sat, Rafael could see Father Stratton, the young man in khaki uniform and another man in the corridor. "Hi, Father."

The stranger took a few steps into the room and stopped. Looking at Rafael, he said, "Yeah. So what?"

The policeman said, "Rafael, this is the driver of the three-thirty bus you say you were on two days ago."

"Two days ago?" the man asked. "Monday? Yeah. This kid was on the bus. Three-thirty run."

"You sure?"

"Sure I'm sure. I know this kid. I put him off at Morgantown. Usually drunk, or as hung-over as an old whore's tits. On the run from the city usually he's sneakin' drinks. I watch him in the rear view mirror. His head bobs up and down behind the seat. Sometimes he falls asleep and I have to pull the bus over at the dump exit and go back and shake him awake and help him off the bus. He's never been any trouble, though. Any real trouble."

"Two days ago. . ." the policeman said. "How do you know he was on the bus Monday?"

"It was Monday," the driver said. "I saw him waitin' outside Freedo's bar and I said to myself, 'Oh, boy, look at that." He was standin' there on the sidewalk with this shoppin' cart full of junk. Jeez, he had dresses, a big, drippin' turkey, and a half-gallon jug of vodka. 'Maybe I'm gonna have trouble with this kid today,' I said to myself. He wanted to bring the shoppin' cart aboard the bus. I said, 'No way, Jose.' I had to wait while he loaded all that stuff aboard the bus. I watched to see how he could manage that big jug of booze, you know, sneak drinks from it, behind the seat. The bottle came on the bus full and left the bus full."

"You let people drink aboard your bus?" the policeman asked.

"Why not? They're not drivin'. Drinkin' is one good reason for takin' the bus. If they're not botherin' anybody. Long as I'm not drinkin'. Hey, listen: what have these people down there got to live for? Dump pickers. They get ahold of a bottle, I say, 'Good luck to 'em.'"

"You picked him up in the city?"

"Yeah. Outside Freedo's, where I usually pick him up."

"Where did he get off?"

"On the highway above Morgantown. Usually I pick those people up and let 'em off at the dump exit, but sometimes, when the traffic's light or they're especially sick or drunk or carryin' groceries or somethin' I pull the bus over as much as I can right above Morgantown and let 'em off. That way all they need do is roll right down the hill. Hey, why not? What have these people got to live for? Might as well make life easy for 'em, I say. You know there are kids down there? Little kids? What a hell hole! What a way to live! You people should do somethin' about it. Really!"

"And you're sure it was Monday afternoon this

kid was aboard your bus with all his packages, the big bottle of vodka. . ."

"Yeah. Monday. That was the day I had to steer the bus through all those cop cars outside that big liquor store in Big Dry Lake. Wasn't a woman killed? Everybody was lookin' out the windows of the bus. Is that what this is about? Yeah, the kid was aboard the bus. I remember lookin' back at everybody gawpin' out the windows at all the police cars. This kid was lookin' out the window. I remember thinkin', 'Big bottle of vodka like that and he's not drinkin' from it. Maybe it's too big for him to lift to his mouth.'"

The policeman sighed. "Okay."

"I can go?"

Father Stratton waved at Rafael through the doorway and left.

The policeman said to the driver, "Thanks for comin' in."

The driver turned to leave the room. "Listen, if my wife calls, you'll tell her why you brought me in?"

"Sure."

"I mean, I'll tell her and all. But if she doesn't believe me. . ."

"Any question, have her call me. No problem."

"I used to drink, myself, but now I've got this job drivin' a bus—"

"I'll talk to her." The policeman continued

holding the door open with his back. "Okay, Rafael. The system works; you'd better believe it. You can go home. Eat fried turkey. Get drunk. Make more babies." To the young man wearing khakis still standing in the corridor, he said, "Check this kid out."

"Yes, sir."

As Rafael was passing the policeman in the doorway, the policeman said, "Tell your brother he's full of shit."

Rita was on a bench in the lobby of the police station. Her face lit like a moon breaking clouds when she saw Rafael. Frankie was on his back gurgling in her lap. Lina lay asleep on the bench beside Rita.

"Hey," Rafael said. "How'd you get here?"

Rita stood, with Frankie in her arms. "Walked in. Figured I'd better see Father Stratton, ask him what to do."

"You walked in, carryin' the kids?"

"We left early. Before it got too hot. Lina walked a little bit of the way."

Rita had a little cut on the tip of her nose, probably from falling face down in the dirt.

"Where's Marta?"

"I told her not to leave Mama's sight. She'll be all right."

"You walked."

The older policeman whistled at Rafael from behind his counter. "Come over here. Sign this."

Standing in front of the counter, Rafael found the counter was chest-high on him. The blue uniformed policeman towered over him. "Sign what?"

"This." The policeman slid a piece of paper across the counter to Rafael. He tried to hand Rafael a pen. "It says we didn't steal nothin' from you or abuse you in any way."

"But you did take something from me," Rafael said.

"What? What did you ever have?"

"You took an important night from me."

"Shit," the policeman said. "Sign this, wise guy, or we'll take another 'important night' from you. Obstructing justice."

Taking the pen, Rafael wrote on the paper R A L.

"What's this?" The policeman turned the paper around on the counter. "Your initials?"

"That's how I sign my name," Rafael said.

"Okay. I get it. That will do, I guess." With the paper in hand, he turned away from Rafael.

Standing beside him, Rita said, "It's real cold in here, Rafael."

Rafael asked the policeman's back: "Aren't you gonna take us home?"

Eyebrows shot up his forehead, the policeman

turned and looked at Rafael. "You want limousine service?"

"You brought me here in a police car."

"Call a taxi."

"I haven't got my boots."

"I'm sorry, Rafael," Rita said softly. "I forgot you didn't have your boots."

"My wife's already walked all the way in here carryin' two kids."

"Call a taxi," the policeman said.

"But I didn't do anything!" Rafael said. "You can ask—"

"Get out of here."

"Hey," Rafael said. "I can't walk all the way home along the highway in the midday-sun carryin' two kids without any boots!"

"Sure you can," the policeman said in a low voice. "You're a tough little Indian, aren't you?"

P

ALESSANDRO'S
mouth was full of turkey. He said, "It's all right."

Just about everyone was there, in the store, late
Wednesday afternoon, eating the turkey dinner:
Rafael's father, Marta, Lina, Nito, Tita, Jazz,
Rocky, Sammy, other kids, Allesandro, Old Callie, Rock, Mrs. Woburn, Marie, Faro, Macky, both
families from the double wide who had provided
the propane gas to fry the turkey once Rita had cut
and broken it into pieces, except Francine, who
was too sick with the cancer to come, or even eat,
Heyman, Rider, Hortense, John Williams, a few
others, more recent arrivals Rafael did not know
too well, Rita with Frankie on her lap. . . Some of
the turkey dinner had been delivered on paper
plates to Mama in bed in her packing crate and to
Ninja on the back seat of the collapsed Cadillac
where he lived now suffering a general fever from
his shot leg.

Luis was not there.

Keeping just enough for bus fare to the city for
himself Thursday, and, for Rita later, Rafael spent
the rest of his money buying the warm beer and

soft drinks from the store for the people eating his turkey.

With Lina on his back, her arms around his neck, Frankie in his arms, that mid-day Rafael had walked barefoot along the edge of the highway from Big Dry Lake to Morgantown. Rita offered to carry one of the children, but Rafael did not let her. She had already carried the two children from Morgantown to Big Dry Lake that morning. The sun broiled them as they walked. The side of the road heated by the sun fried the soles of Rafael's bare feet, made them increasingly sensitive to the stones he could not avoid.

Because of the heat, because Rita had walked that distance carrying the children already that day, because Rafael had not slept all night shivering from the cold in the jail, they stopped frequently on the walk, wherever there was shade not far from their path, and cooled and rested themselves and the children as much as possible.

At first on the highway, Rafael had turned to face the traffic and, walking backwards, one baby on his back, another held on one arm, he stuck out his right hand with the thumb up to ask for a ride but no one stopped or even slowed. He knew they looked what they were, a poor, sweaty, dirty, probably smelly young family with no place real to go, nothing sexy or otherwise interesting about them, and very possibly a potential burden. After a while he gave up trying to get them a ride and just trudged slowly. Pain from his bare feet shot up his legs at every step.

The walk took much longer than usual.

By the time they arrived in Morgantown the skin of the bottom of Rafael's feet had been pretty well cooked and cut off him.

As they were coming down the sloped dirt track from the dump exit off the highway, Rafael saw Rocky dash into the store.

In a moment, Rafael's brother, Luis, came out of the store.

Luis stood in the sunlight, on the dry earth outside the store. He squinted through the strong sunlight up the track at his approaching brother.

Rafael could see the top of his brother's stomach begin to pump as Luis grabbed in short, shallow breaths.

Luis ran to his pick up truck parked in the shade. He started the engine with a roar. The rear tires of the truck skidded in the soft dirt before they gained traction. The back of the truck slid sideways. When the truck was pointed at Rafael, Rita, Lina and Marta, up the track toward the highway, it accelerated rapidly. The rear wheels spun up dirt.

Rafael and Rita jumped aside as the truck headed for them.

The truck passed them with a roar.

Its tires digging into the track raised a huge cloud of dust.

As the dust settled on them, Rita and the children coughed.

Rafael could see little through the dust. He heard from the place where the dump track joined the highway car horns blaring and the screachings of more than one set of brakes.

He guessed Luis had just bounced and slammed his truck onto the highway indifferent to traffic.

Rafael did not hear the sound of metal crunching, glass smashing, that would have meant an accident.

As they were passing her crate, Mama shouted through her window, "Rafael, I knew you did no such bad thing!"

"I didn't, Mama!"

"Was that Luis' truck I heard, leaving?"

"Yes, Mama."

"That boy had better make himself scarce around here!" Her several skin chins seemed to get larger. "I get my hands on that boy. . ."

Rafael cut his eyes sideways to Rita, to see if she, too, was smiling.

Rita asked, "You'll have some turkey, Mama, when it's ready?"

"I've been living for it!" Mama said.

Rita went to the stream and carried back two buckets of water herself.

Returning to the trailer, first she cooled the children by washing them down with wet rags. She told them they must stay out of the sun for the rest of the day. She fed the children and gave them water to drink.

Rafael sat on their single-sized bunk. His bare feet dangled in the air above the floor. The bubbling sweat on his torso caused by walking, carrying the children in the sun, dried. A different sweat from the air inside the sun heated trailer cooled his body.

Rita placed the second bucket of water near Rafael's feet.

Kneeling before him, with the rags, the water, she cleaned Rafael's feet. "This is terrible," she said.

"It's not important."

With a little scissors, Rita cut away some of the skin, trimmed the gashes on the soles of his feet.

Rafael said, "Ow."

"I don't mean to hurt you."

"I know."

Doing the best she could with the wet rags she had, she wrapped his feet, making knots around his ankles.

"These will take a long time to heal," she said.

"That'll be all right."

"Maybe you should try to keep these rags wet awhile."

"Is that the best thing to do?"

"I don't know. I'll ask old Callie. I think the bandages wet would be more comfortable for you."

"I want to sleep in the hammock," Rafael said.

"And I," Rita said, rising from the floor, smiling, "will get that turkey cooked!"

Rafael stood gingerly on his feet wrapped in wet rags. "Is there other food to go with it?"

"Cereal."

"That would be good. Warm food?"

"We cannot ask people to use too much of their propane, you know?"

She poured the bucket of bloody water out the door of the trailer.

Later in the afternoon, Rita awakened Rafael in the hammock.

"The turkey is cooked," she said.

"Where are the kids?"

She held Frankie in her arms. "At the store. They have been very interested in seeing the turkey broken apart and fried, excited by what it will taste like." She laughed. "Everyone is at the store."

"Is Luis?" Rafael asked.

"No. Luis has not come back."

Making her own surprise, Rita had stirred some water into dry cereal and bread crumbs and left it in the sun an hour or two to bake or, at least, to warm. At the last minute, she poured grease from the frying pans in which the various pieces of the tur-

key had been cooked over it. "Like a dressing!"
She said. "A stuffing! Is that right?"

Mrs. Woburn shared a pound of potato salad she
had bought in a Big Dry Lake store the day before.

Faro and the boy who now lived with her,
Macky, had made cole slaw for everyone. They
chopped up all the cabbage and onions they could
find, and added canned carrots and beans. They
used a whole bottle of salad dressing on it.

Everyone in the store, even the children, ate all
this food in silence.

When they were done eating, there was no more
food left.

Old Callie went to the counter. She inspected the
various turkey bones. "Maybe I could make a soup
of that."

Quietly, Rita said, "The children are real tired."

"Do you think they will sleep?" Rafael grinned.

"I know they will."

As she sat on the floor, her back against a box,
Lina's stomach actually protruded. Her chin was
falling onto her collar bone.

"They have had a long day," Rita said. "How
do you feel?" she asked Rafael.

"Fine. I slept."

"You know what I mean," Rita said.

Rafael said, "You know what I mean."

Rita stood up. "I will put the children in their
beds."

After Rita left with the children, Rafael remained sitting. He looked around at the quiet group in the store. They had been well fed. No one seemed to be looking at each other, or at him. Their stomachs, their whole bodies had been surprised by plenty of good food, including turkey, which many had not tasted before. It was as if their bodies, their minds were in a state of shock. They were feeling their stomachs full. Maybe they were concentrating on their digesting all this food. Maybe some of them, the older ones especially, were remembering other big meals they had had, other groups with whom they had eaten well. Would they remember this? Rafael wondered. *Please remember this*, Rafael thought. *Please remember what I have tried to say to you. . .*

After a moment, Rafael stretched and stood up on his bandaged feet.

Without saying anything, Rafael limped to the door.

"Rafael," his father said.

Rafael stopped near his father's chair.

"Rafael," his father said. "Do not kill your brother."

Rafael looked outside the door. There was still plenty of light left in the day. "Luis?" Rafael said. "No."

q

IN THE heat of the late
afternoon in their single bunk in their travel trailer,
Rita and Rafael made love softly, slowly, sweetly.

Their children, Lina, Marta, Frankie were asleep
in their various beds in the little trailer.

All Morgantown was quiet.

Rita said to Rafael, "Naked, with your feet
bound up that way in wet rags, you look like some
kind of sexy boy pictured in a magazine. Do your
feet sting much?"

"It's not important."

"But, do they?"

"A little."

"The turkey was wonderful."

"Did you get enough of it?"

"Oh, yes."

Together they slept for awhile.

It was still light when he moved against her.

She said, "You seem so healthy, now."

He said, "I'm good."

Again, quietly, they loved each other.

"I'd like to stay here," Rita said. "Until the
children wake up."

"Okay."

"Are you getting up?"

"I slept this afternoon."

"You go to your job tomorrow."

"Yes."

"Your new clothes are all clean."

"I saw them on the clothes line. I don't know when you had time to wash them."

Rita said, "It is hard to get blood out of clothes."

"I'm sure they're fine."

"I want you to look nice," Rita said, "when you go to your job tomorrow."

Rafael put his feet on the floor and waited a moment before standing on them.

Rita rolled onto her side and settled her face on the pillow.

She said, "What I meant about your father. . . I'm sorry for him. I'm sorry for you. I'm sorry for everybody. But it is no tragedy. Do you know what I mean?"

Rafael said, "Yes. I guess so."

r

RAFAEL SET a match to the papers and kindling and wood he had piled on a bare spot of earth in a dead woods downstream well out of sight of Morgantown, beyond the end of the dump fence. Around the pile he had made a circle of stones. The fire he built was a meter from the stream. He had gathered enough wood to last him the night.

Sitting on his heels, he watched the fire spread to its edges, find itself contained by the circle of stones, grow up to catch the dry logs on top.

Night fell to full dark.

Standing then, a lone figure moving around his fire in the dark night, Rafael took off everything he was wearing, except the rags binding his feet.

Rafael crouched again. With his cupped hands, he scooped up the dirt of the earth and poured it over his head. He scooped more and poured it over each shoulder, each thigh.

Standing then, with the palms of his hands he rubbed the dirt against his skin, his face, shoulders, down his arms, across his chest, his stomach, on the small of his back, down every side of his legs.

As the moon broke over the hill its light filtered through the heavy, warm air to where Rafael stood by his fire.

Feeling the dirt caked on the sweat drying on his skin, Rafael walked around his fire. The first time he circled the fire, he looked down at it, seeing it from all sides, the yellow flames on top, the red embers below. The second time, he looked to the sky and saw the stars fading against the light of the rising moon. The third time, he studied his own shadows, one from the fire, the other from the moon, how they lengthened and shortened, darkened and dimmed, moved in relation to each other and to him, in these uncertain lights.

Gingerly on his cut, bandaged feet Rafael went down the short bank of the stream. He sat in the water. His head upstream, he laid himself fully in the stream, his legs straight, his back and the back of his head on the stream bottom. The sluggish, oily water washed down his body. His fingers shook the dirt out of his hair. His hands then brushed the caked dirt off his skin. He rolled onto his stomach. Face down in the water, he felt the water flow over his shoulders, down his back, down the back of his legs.

When he stood up in the stream, he felt the night air cooler against his skin. He spread his legs. He lifted his arms. He concentrated on the air against every part of his body.

Standing by his fire, his arms raised, he rotated slowly. He watched the bubbles of water dry on his skin. He felt the dry heat of the fire sharpen as his body dried.

About once an hour during that night, Rafael similarly bathed himself in the stream, felt the night air against his freshened skin, dried himself by the fire.

Each time he sat by the fire, he sat in a different place. Half the times, he sat facing the fire, seeing it from a new angle. He held sticks to the fire, watched them smoke, then glow, flame, turn to ash, be consumed. He watched sparks from some of the bigger pieces of wood burst up from the fire, rise into the air above his head, extinguish. Half the times he sat with his back to the fire, looking out into the night, each time from a different angle. He watched the moonlight and the shadows it caused move on the silent earth.

From nearby, he could hear the crackling, shifting fire. From afar, he could hear the cars and trucks on the highway.

Many times during that night as he sat by his fire, Rafael inhaled deeply, through his mouth, then only through his nose, filling his lungs with the heavy air, exhaling slowly. Each time he did this, he sent his tongue around his mouth, trying to clean out, spit out the metallic taste.

As daylight grayed the eastern sky, Rafael

bathed one final time. After drying himself by the fire, feeling its heat one last time, he took the fire apart. He threw the smoldering, burning pieces of wood into the stream where they extinguished with a hiss.

Rafael dressed.

Standing one last moment by his smoldering fire, Rafael found the spent cigarette lighter in the pocket of his jeans. He dropped it on the ashes.

Thinking of Rita and his children and breakfast, Rafael limped up the path broken by discarded things along the stream to Morgantown.

It had been a short summer's night.

S

"YOU ARE eating so much," Rita said. "I have never seen you eat so much breakfast."

Sitting cross-legged on the floor of the travel trailer with Lina and Marta, Rafael was eating his third bowl of cereal and water that morning. He had had two cups of condensed milk and water and now was drinking a cup of powdered coffee and water.

From her nearby trailer, Faro's portable radio was blaring dance music.

With big gestures, Lina was showing how well she could eat her cereal from a bowl with a spoon. Marta was trying to imitate her, but each time her spoon approached her mouth it tipped and her wet cereal fell to her legs or the floor.

Putting aside his own bowl, Rafael scooped Marta into the lap created by his crossed legs. He took her bowl and her spoon and began to feed her. She kept her own fist around the handle of her spoon as Rafael filled it with cereal and guided it to her mouth.

As she ate, Marta looked victoriously at her sister.

"You did not take the early bus," Rita said.

"I don't have to be there until eleven," Rafael said.

"When you did not come home last night . . ."

"I'm fine."

When Marta's bowl was empty but her mouth still full, she pulled her spoon entirely away from Rafael. She began tapping her spoon against her bowl in rhythm to the loud music she heard through the windows and door of the trailer.

Rafael laughed.

Keeping Marta in the diamond of his legs, Rafael reached behind him. He snapped open the doors to the cabinet beneath the dry sink. He pulled out two metal cooking pots. He put one upside down on the floor in front of Lina and one upside down in front of himself.

With his spoon he began drumming the overturned cooking pot in rhythm with the music from Faro's radio, matching the exact clinking Marta was making with her spoon against her bowl. Marta giggled and began hitting her bowl harder.

With her spoon, Lina hit the pot Rafael had overturned in front of her and the bowl next to it alternately.

Rafael noticed that Marta stopped using her spoon and her bowl for rhythm. Instead she was hitting her bowl in different places with her spoon, each hit producing a different note. She was imitating the melody of the song.

Laughing, Rafael double-timed the rhythm with his spoon and pot. For variation, he double-timed the rhythm against his bowl.

Before leaving the trailer to get Rafael's clothes from the drying line, Rita stood a moment looking down at her family sitting on the floor, Rafael and Marta and Lina, making this extraordinary noise, attempting rhythms and melodies by hitting spoons against metal cooking pots and cereal bowls, nearly drowning out the music from the radio that had started them off. Now they were making their own melodies and rhythms oblivious of the radio dance music. Lina was giggling. Marta was laughing outright. Rafael was laughing so hard his eyes were wet. Rita shook her head in wonder, and smiled, loving them all so much she felt her heart swell.

When she returned, with Rafael's new shirt and jeans over her arm, they had stopped their noise.

Both daughters were in the diamond formed by Rafael's crossed legs. Nuzzling the neck of one, then the other, Rafael hugged both daughters to him tightly.

When Rafael looked up at Rita she saw an expression on his face she was not sure she had ever seen before, on anyone. Lively, his face radiated the greatest love and happiness.

Rita said, "I figure you can wear two pairs of socks in your boots to make it easier on your cut-up feet."

"Okay."

Gently, Rafael lifted his two daughters off his legs and sat them on the floor.

Before taking his clothes from Rita, Rafael went to the box where Frankie gurgled. Rafael picked the baby up, swung him over his head. He hugged Frankie to his chest and kissed the top of his head.

He hugged the baby only an instant before putting him back on the rags in his cradle box.

Rafael did not turn around when Rita tried to hand him the two pairs of balled grayed white socks. She could not see his face. She dropped the socks on their bed.

The jeans and shirt he put on were a little stiff but they were warm from hanging from the line in the morning sun.

As he pulled on his boots over the two pairs of socks, Rafael said, "Okay."

"That'll be easier for you," Rita said.

"Yes."

"More comfortable."

"Thanks."

In the door of the trailer, Rita hugged Rafael's neck. "Bye."

Rafael hugged Rita. He kissed her face. He said, "Remember."

t

MAMA CALLED
through her window to Rafael as he came along the
dirt track. "Are you going to work now, Rafael?"

"Yes, Mama."

"Are you late?"

"No, Mama."

"I thought when you did not come back you
had gone out and gotten drunk last night and you
would not know what you were doing this morning. I was afraid you would miss your job."

"I know what I'm doing this morning, Mama."

"Do well, Rafael."

Passing the store, Rafael heard people inside but
did not look to see who was there.

Walking along the track to the highway's dump
exit where the bus to the city would stop for him,
the sun on Rafael's shoulders, through his new,
washed shirt, felt good.

Rafael's brother, Luis, was coming down the
track.

Luis was walking unevenly, as if fighting a
strong wind. Some of his steps were to the side; a
few were backward. If there had been consistent

rhythm to his movements he might have been dancing. At one point, his body rushed to the side, his feet hurrying to stay under his weight.

In his right hand, carried by the neck, was a quart bottle of beer. What beer was left in the bottle was foaming from the heat, from his movements.

Rafael was close to his brother before Luis saw him, recognized him.

It took Luis a moment to focus on Rafael's face.

"Rafael," Luis announced. "I am drunk."

"That's okay," Rafael said.

"Very, very drunk."

"Okay."

"I wrecked the truck."

"That's okay."

"Totally wrecked the truck."

"Okay."

"I got very, very drunk and the truck went off the road and the wheels caught in a ditch and rolled over and over. I totally wrecked it."

"That's okay, Luis."

"I thought you did it. I thought you killed that woman in the liquor store."

"I didn't."

"The presents. The food. The new clothes. The big bottle of vodka."

"Why didn't you ask me?"

"What would you have have said?"

"I would have said, Why are you asking me?"

"I'm sorry, bro'. . ."

"That's okay."

"Where are you going now?"

"City."

Standing near the highway in the dirt road to the dump in the bright morning sunlight, Rafael did not have to wait long for the bus.

As the bus climbed the highway along the shoulder of the hill, Rafael looked through the bus window at Morgantown slipping below, behind him. The people were moving around there as they would any other day.

Rafael saw his father going through the gap in the fence into the dump.

Under the top sheet of the bed Rita and he had shared in the travel trailer Rafael had put the bank book, the bank signature card, bus fare to the city, and the contract:

Raphaël

$250

$300

$50

$250

$29,700.00

$29,700.00

Thursday 11. A.M.

RAEL

Morroco

WORKS BY GREGORY MCDONALD

Fletch
Confess, Fletch
Fletch's Fortune
Fletch and The Widow Bradley
Fletch's Moxie
Fletch and The Man Who
Carioca Fletsh
Fletch Won
Fletch, Too

Flynn
The Buck Passes Flynn
Flynn's In

Running Scared
Safekeeping
Love Among The Mashed Potatoes (Dear M.E.)
Who Took Tony Rinaldi?
The Brave

Time².
Exits and Entrances
Merely Players
A World Too Wide

NON-FICTION

The Education of Gregory Macdonald

DRAMA

Bull's Eye